FACING UP

by Robin F. Brancato

ALFRED A. KNOPF   NEW YORK

THIS IS A BORZOI BOOK
PUBLISHED BY ALFRED A. KNOPF, INC.

2   4   6   8   0   9   7   5   3   1
Manufactured in the United States of America

Library of Congress Cataloging in Publication Data
Brancato, Robin F.   Facing up.
Summary: After a high school love triangle explodes in
deceit and tragedy, a young man confronts his complicity
in the death of his best friend.
[1. High schools—Fiction.   2. Schools—Fiction.
3. Friendship—Fiction   4. Death—Fiction]   I. Title.
PZ7.B73587Fac   1984   [Fic]   83-18708
ISBN 0-394-85488-8   ISBN 0-394-95488-2 (lib. bdg.)

FOR JOHN

FACING UP

1

Dave bounces his knees up and down under the desk. Hurry, Jepson, if you're going to pull this off. Only fifteen more minutes to go in the last period of the day. Jep's seat in the front row has been empty from the start. Now or never, Dave thinks as he looks around the room.

Schultz, the health teacher, is really into the heart of the lecture now. He's holding up the guts of the Visible Man model and reminding them for the hundredth time that *You are what you eat.* Meanwhile, over by the window, big Willoughby—Willo—is squirming in a desk chair that's much too small for him. Dave catches Willo's eye.

Willo forms the words silently: *What's happening with Jepson?*

Dave shrugs and glances at the girl sitting next to him. Nan something—Tobin, that's it. She just came from California. Must be rough to come all the way to Long Island in the middle of your junior year. She's writing again, he sees—filling a whole page up.

Then his eyes come to rest where they usually do, on Susan. This is one of two classes with her and the best one for watching. She's running a comb through her dark-blond wavy hair—right out in the open, not caring what anybody thinks. Face it, she's vain, but she's got reason to be. Name one guy in this room who hasn't had a thing for her at some point. Lately people are saying she's just playing around with Jepson.

Susan turns and crosses her legs so that Dave feels light-headed. Cool it. Forget it. *She's going with your best friend.*

True. Best friend for a year at least. Dave smiles at the thought of how much in awe of Jep he used to be. It must have been Jep's height and full mustache in ninth grade that did it. Plus his nerve, and his humor, of course.

The wall intercom buzzes. Dave sits up.

Desk chairs creak. Someone laughs. Willo looks at Dave. Schultz, setting down a plastic pancreas, makes his way toward the wall speaker. He presses the button.

"Yes, what is it?"

A male voice comes through the heavy crackle of static. *"Mr. Schultz?"*

"Yes?"

Dave bites his cheeks to make sure he won't laugh.

"The inspector came sooner than we expected today. He's checking certain rooms for asbestos in the ceiling tile. Please help us out by dismissing your class."

Schultz's jowls sag. "Now, you mean?"

"Yes, please, immediately." The voice and static fade away.

Schultz scowls.

A cresendo of sound builds—talking, scraping of chairs. Dave watches Susan whisper to the kid next to her.

"Wait. Wait a minute!" Schultz hovers in the doorway. "Don't think you're getting off that easy! A quiz on the gastrointestinal tract the next time you come!" Then he opens the door and the students rush out.

Dave, in the hall, sees Willo beside him. "Asbestos," he chuckles. "Jepson does it again."

"Was that him?" Willo says. "I swear he sounded like Richards. How'd he get *in* there?"

"Charmed his way, I guess. Where're you headed?"

"My locker for a second."

"See you later." Dave spots Susan outside the double doors.

"You know why Jep did that?" Susan grins as Dave joins her. "I could only get an appointment at Hairways at two-fifteen. Jep said, 'No problem, you'll be there on time.' Isn't he something else?"

"Yeah." They go outside. The sun is out and the air smells like spring. "You're getting your hair cut?" Dave asks.

"I don't know." Susan looks up. "Think I should?"

"No," Dave says. "I mean—how do *you* like it?"

"Don't worry." She nudges him with her elbow. "I'm only getting a trim. You like long hair, don't you?"

"Yeah." Especially on you, he should say. He wishes he was better at talking to girls.

Susan waves to someone in a car and then says to Dave, "Listen, so long. I'm getting a ride. Tell Jep he did great getting us out of class. I'll see you later."

"You will?"

"Didn't Jep tell you? My friend Mindy's having a party tonight. Her parents are in Europe and her brother won't be home. Willo said he'd drive us." Susan turns so that the wind swirls her hair. "You *have* to come," she says.

"Okay, I will." Dave follows her with his eyes until she gets into the car and the driver pulls away. Now to find Jepson. Dave glances across the street. There he is, in the parking lot, sitting on the fender of Willo's Chevy, with Willo, Bull Curtis, and Mazur all gathered around. Dave hurries over.

"How'd you get his voice right?" Willo is asking Jepson.

Jep hunches. "No sweat. I've been practicing two years."

"The secretary didn't see you when you picked up the microphone?"

"Nope." Jep brushes his mustache. "Out to lunch, as they say." Looking up, he opens his arms when he sees Dave. "Hey, Jacoby, my main man!"

Dave smiles. "Guess what? Some guy is in there ripping the ceiling tile out of Schultz's room."

Jep laughs. "About time. Have you noticed what that asbestos is doing to the Visible Man? He looks terminal. Hey, let's get moving, okay?" Jep lowers himself to the ground and heads toward his Moped. "Who besides Jacoby's coming over to my house?"

"Can't," Mazur answers.

Bull Curtis shakes his head. "Sorry, got to work. So long, see you tonight."

Jep, unlocking his Moped, straddles the seat. "Dave and I could use some help on this April Fool's thing we're planning. Willo?"

"Wish I could," Willo says. "I got baseball practice." He stands by his car, chewing a wad of gum. "Changed your mind, Jacoby? Think you might come out for baseball?"

"No," Dave says.

Willo shifts awkwardly. "It was more fun with us both out."

Dave hesitates. "Yeah, it was good. You'll like it though, once you start playing games."

"I guess so." Willo edges slowly toward the car door. "Want a lift? I don't have to be on the field for another fifteen minutes."

"No, thanks," Dave says. Jep's Moped is circling around him. "I'm going to hop on the back here. See you later, right?"

"Yeah," Willo calls. "I'm picking you guys up tonight!"

Dave jumps on the Moped as Jepson takes off. Knees out and feet balanced, they bump across the lot.

"Hang on, man!" Jep calls.

"So long!" Dave calls to Willo. Clinging to the Moped with both hands, he bounces as they go down the parking-lot ramp. Dave turns to look at a dark-haired girl crossing at Harrison Street. Nan from health class. He nods and she smiles and waves. Not Susan, but not bad. He frees one hand to wave back at her.

Feels good to be moving. Dave breathes in fresh air. A warm day for the end of March. This should be a great spring.

"Still there?" Jep yells as he rushes to beat a red light.

"Yeah, yeah," Dave says. "You can't lose me that easy!"

2

Jep, lifting the black netting that makes a tent around the bed, settles himself on the mattress on the floor of his bedroom. "How about this headline for the April Fool's paper: SCHULTZ BLAMES MORAL DECAY OF STUDENTS ON CAFETERIA FOOD. HEALTH TEACHER CLAIMS YOU ARE WHAT YOU EAT?"

"Yeah, that's good," Dave says. "How about VISIBLE MAN TO RECEIVE LIVER TRANSPLANT?"

"Great. Got the sodas?"

"Here." Handing two cans under the netting, Dave crawls under and joins Jep, so that both of them are sitting on the mattress on the floor.

"Corn chips?" Jep offers.

"Thanks. How about this?" Dave asks. "PAUL JEPSON EXPELLED FOR PULLING OFF ASBESTOS HOAX."

"Forget that one," Jep says. He dips into the bag of chips. "And forget the 'Paul,' too. One name from my old man is enough."

Dave reaches into the bag. "Do you ever see your father?"

Jep, shaking his head, chews distractedly for a moment. Running his hand through his black, curly hair, he sniffs and sits up suddenly. "Back to work," he says. "Come on, only four days till April Fool's Day. Looks like you and I are going to end up writing the whole damned thing. What'll we call it?"

Dave considers. "How about *Bel-Hi Carrion* instead of *Clarion*. Carrion means dead and putrefying flesh."

"I know what it means, man. *Word Power,* Lesson Six." Jep opens the sodas. *"Bell-Hi Carrion.* Not bad." He hands Dave a foaming can.

Dave tilts it to his lips. "How's it going to be printed?"

Jep takes a long swallow. "My mother'll make Xerox copies at her office. You type up the original."

"I type lousy."

"Better than I do."

"Who's taking notes on all this, anyway?" Dave asks.

Jep gets up. "You are, while I take a leak."

As Jep disappears on the other side of the netting, Dave jots notes in ink on the back of his hand. Then he looks around Jep's room. Some great concept, he thinks. Funny, how he wasn't sure how it would turn out when Jep first thought it up. Black walls and black see-through material draped to form a tent over the mattress. "What's the point?" he had asked him then.

"Privacy," Jep said.

"You got it *anyway,*" Dave told him. "Nobody's ever home at your house."

"Atmosphere, then. It looks like a harem."

"You'll invite Susan up?" Dave remembers asking.

"Hell, yeah, she'll be first."

Dave glances around now at the fake oriental rug hanging on the wall and the Indian-print spread. Behind him are posters of Jim Morrison and Jimi Hendrix. Dave's been thinking he's going to try something like this with his room at home.

Jep comes back now, zipping his jeans and crawling

into the tent again. "So where were we?" he asks. "How about BELLE PARK PRINCIPAL TIED TO MAFIA? 'The body of B. F. Richards, corrupt high school principal, was found yesterday hanging from a meat hook in the home ec room.'"

Dave coughs so that a trickle of soda runs down his chin. "That's what they'll do to us when they catch us selling the *Carrion.*"

Jep settles back on the mattress again. "Hell, no. This is clean fun. They should give us a service award for this."

Dave reaches for more corn chips. "You're not worried about the asbestos thing?"

Jep crosses his eyes. "What, me worry, you kidding?"

Dave stops chewing. "Don't you ever? I don't mean about stuff like this, I mean big stuff—about, like, *dying,* say."

Jep dips into the bag again. "I look at it this way. What's the worst that can happen?" He smiles ironically. "You *taste it* and spend eternity with Hendrix and Morrison."

"Taste it?"

"Bite the dust." Jep crunches noisily. "Get blown away, kick the bucket."

"And that doesn't worry you . . ."

Jep glances at the posters. "If those guys are there—wherever *there* is—how bad could it be?" He tosses a corn-chip at Dave across the mattress. "Come on, cut the heavy stuff. How about a sports story? WILLO SIGNED BY YANKEE FARM CLUB. 'Big Bill Willoughby, ace catcher for Belle Park, was signed yesterday by the Beachport, Maine, 4-H Club. Willoughby's primary duty will be to transport manure from one Yankee farm to another.'"

Dave coughs again. "Yeah, good. We need one about Susan. SUSAN SCHERRA WINS BROOKE SHIELDS LOOK-ALIKE CONTEST."

Jep nods. "She'd go for that."

Dave looks up cautiously. "Think she's better-looking than Shields?"

"Hard to compare. Susan's earthier."

"Meaning what?"

"Meaning *more animal.*"

"Yeah?" Dave forces a smile.

"She may be coming over tonight, before the party," Jep says, touching his mustache.

"Yeah?" Dave clears his throat. "Got anything special planned?"

"Sure. Candles, incense, The Doors on the stereo . . ."

"Let me know how it goes." Dave's mind drifts for a minute. "You're so damned lucky," he says finally, "I can see *me* bringing Susan home."

Jep drains his soda. "Why, what would happen?"

"For starters," Dave says, "we'd never make it upstairs. My mother'd be stopping us in the kitchen with cookies and milk. My father'd be giving me this *watch it, man* look that says '*I* never got away with that stuff, so don't think *you're* going to, either!' If we actually made it all the way to my bedroom, my sister would be shooting Polaroids through the keyhole."

Jep snorts. "You got a tough life, Jacoby, a real tough life. I never knew anybody until you who's got such a normal family. Hang loose, man. You'll be on your own soon. Then you can get kinky."

"Another whole year and a half until college."

"You'll live."

"In a fishbowl."

Jep stretches his legs. "Don't sweat it. School'll be over in a couple of months. We could work at a resort this summer."

"I already tried that idea."

"And?"

" 'Wait till you're eighteen,' my parents said. They want me to work at home."

"This summer? Doing what?"

"On the assembly line at Brite-Lite, the flashlight place. My dad knows somebody. Sounds beat, doesn't it?"

Jep thinks for a second. "Not if I was there. Could your father put in a word for me?"

"Maybe. I'll ask him."

"We could keep each other awake."

"And hang out after work. What's Susan going to be doing?" Dave asks.

"Staying wherever I am, I hope." Jep chuckles. "Don't worry, we'll find you somebody—some earthy wench on the assembly line."

Dave finishes off the corn chips. "How'll we get to work, in our Porsche?"

"No, in the Jaguar."

"Seriously," Dave says, "let's buy a car. Together, I mean. Share the expenses."

Jep rolls his eyes. "Don't I wish. Fixing up the harem really broke me. I'd love to get a car, but I'm down to my last buck."

"I'll lend you your half. You can pay me back when you start to work."

Jep lifts his eyes. "You'd lend me, no kidding? It'd be great to get mobilized." He leans back on his pillow. "We could take trips all the time, like the one we took on the train last year. I swear that trip to Montauk was one of the greatest things in my life. Remember the waves in that crazy place we had to climb to get down to?"

"Yeah, they're best at the end of summer."

"So that's when we'll go there."

"You and me?" Dave asks.

"Who else? Load up with six-packs, camp out—"

"Leave Susan at home?"

"Absence'll make her heart grow fonder. Let's definitely do it, okay?"

"Sure," Dave says. "All we need is the car."

Jep reaches into the drawer of the table by his bed. "Don't sweat details," he says. "We've got time to work it out. Want to smoke?" he asks, rolling a paper.

"Not now," Dave says. "I've got to go in a minute."

Jep strikes a match. "Where'd we leave off with the *Carrion*?"

Dave looks at the writing on his hand. "WILLO SIGNED BY YANKEE FARM CLUB."

Jep throws his head back. "Sure you don't want to smoke?"

"No, I've got to go home."

"Don't. We got more work to do."

"I'll come back tomorrow," Dave says. "My mother goes nuts if I don't show for dinner. Want to eat over at my house?"

"No, thanks." Jep inhales. "Susan's coming."

Dave gets up. "What's this party tonight?"

"Mindy's. We'll come for you around eight o'clock." Jep inhales again. "Mind letting yourself out?"

Dave lifts the netting. "No problem. Where's your mother?"

"She's going to Washington, D.C., for the weekend."

"Oh. Okay, see you later. Have—" Dave hesitates. "Have fun with Susan the Animal." Then with a last look backward he makes his way out of the apartment into the hall. It must be great having a place to yourself, nobody else around all weekend. He'd be jealous as hell if it were anyone but Jep.

3

Dave, slipping in the back door, sees that they've started eating. He takes off his jacket and sits at the table. "Hi."

"Hi." His sister Lisa stares at the writing on the back of his hand. "Yuck. What are those marks?"

Dave glances down. "Notes for something," he says. Meanwhile his mom is looking at him like he's the Elephant Man. "Sorry I'm late. I got a little delayed."

"Serve yourself when you're late!" Lisa gloats.

"I'll get it for him this time." His mother gets up.

"Let him get it, Mary," his father says.

"Yeah, let me—" Dave says half-heartedly, sinking back in his seat.

His dad's mouth is full. "Did they keep you late at practice?"

"Practice? Not exactly—"

Lisa's eyes dart from Dave to her father. "He's not playing baseball this year. Didn't he tell you?"

"He told me," his mother says, putting his plate down in front of him.

His dad looks up from his dinner. "How's that, no baseball?"

Dave stabs a potato. "I've got other stuff to do."

"Oh?" His dad shrugs. "What is it you're doing?"

Dave puts the potato down again. "I'm working on this newspaper."

"*The Clarion*?" Lisa asks.

"Not the *Clarion*, a parody. A mock-out for April Fool's Day. Keep it quiet—it's anonymous."

Dave's father looks at him puzzled. "You're playing an April Fool's joke instead of baseball?"

"Yeah, well, I'll still play ball for fun once in a while."

"It's not fun on the team?"

"Not as much. It's too organized."

"What's wrong with that?" his dad asks. "What will you have to show for this other thing you're doing?"

"To show who?"

"The colleges you apply to next year, I'm talking about."

Dave sighs. "I'm not doing what I'm doing just to get into college."

"The stronger your record," his mom says, "the more choices you'll have."

"By the way," Lisa interrupts, "I saw you with Susan Scherra this afternoon. How come you got out early?"

Dave tries to keep his face blank. "We got dismissed for an asbestos inspection. Why, where were you spying from?"

"I was looking out of algebra."

"No wonder you flunked the last test."

"She's already made it up, Dave." His mom folds her napkin and lays it on the table. "Don't make her feel bad about that. What's this project you're working on?"

"A mock newspaper for April Fool's Day."

His dad shakes his head. "To each his own. I would have given my right arm at your age to play on a team."

"Your right arm!" Lisa groans. "You wouldn't have made it as an amputee athlete, Daddy!"

Smiling at her, he goes on to Dave, "The main thing I feel seriously is, I'd like to see you accomplishing something. If baseball's not your thing, maybe you should think about a part-time job."

"I am. A job at Brite-Lite."

His father nods approvingly. "Good. Maybe Fred Staller can start you soon."

"Great." Dave clears his throat. He'll wait a while to ask about Jep's job.

Lisa twirls the silver bracelet on her arm. "What are you going to do with the money you make?"

"Buy a car, maybe." His parents are giving him the eye. "What's wrong with having my own car?" he asks.

His mom folds her arms. "You know how I feel about it."

How could he not know? She's told him a million times at least.

"We live six blocks from the school," she says.

"*You* drive when you go six blocks!"

"Sure, to pick up groceries."

Lisa flutters her eyes. "He's got pickups to make, too. *Susan Scherra—*"

"She's going with Jepson, you re-tard!"

"Another thing," his mom goes on. "I've been driving for over twenty years. You've had a license only two months."

"That's why I need a car—to get the experience."

His mom lets out her breath. "You have a lifetime to get that."

"What are you worrying about, my grades? I'll keep up my grades, I swear."

"You'd better," his dad says, "car or no car." Pushing

back his chair, he lays his hands on the table. "Look, there's just one point there that no one has mentioned. Cars *cost.*"

"I've got almost a thousand bucks in the bank."

"You'll be glad for it," his mom says, "when you go off to college."

Lisa stops twirling her bracelet. "We have to pay our own college? I don't think I'll go, then."

"Extras," her mother says wearily.

Dave's father leans forward. "If you spend less than a thousand dollars, you'll be buying yourself a headache. Not to mention the insurance at your age, with an old car."

"I'll be working."

"Dave," his mom says, "Dad didn't have a car of his own until he was twenty-three."

His father waves a hand. "That was a whole different ball game. I was living in the city, Mary. I don't blame him for wanting a car. It just isn't practical moneywise."

"Willo's got one," Dave says.

"Good for him." His dad, stretching, pushes his chair back.

"Is Jep getting a car?" his mom asks.

Dave hesitates. "Yeah, he might. What's that got to do with it?"

"I just wondered where you got the idea."

"Why, don't you think I have ideas of my own?"

"Oh, I'm sure you do. It's just that sometimes I worry about your being influenced by your friends."

"I am not!"

His mom looks at his dad. "Remember when he was ten and never gave us a hard time?"

"Unlike this one here," his dad says, poking Lisa in the ribs.

Lisa, rising, pokes him back. She turns to Dave as she leaves the kitchen. "See? You should've *started out* being a pest, like I did. That way nobody expects you to be any other way."

Dave, slumping, watches her go. Damn it, she's got a point.

"Didn't you forget something?" her mother calls to Lisa.

"Oh, yeah." Lisa's singsong drifts down from upstairs. "May I pleased be excused?"

"What else?"

"It's not *my* night to clear."

"Yes it is," Dave calls back.

"I did it for you Wednesday!"

"You owed me!" Dave shouts.

His dad's getting up now and loosening his tie. "Excuse me, I'm going to catch the end of the news. I'll give Fred Staller a call tonight, Dave, to see what he can do for you over at Brite-Lite."

"Thanks."

Dave's mom begins clearing. "That'll be good, if you're set for the summer. Maybe you'll be able to take some time off at the end and come with us on a trip. We're thinking about going to one of those golf resorts in North Carolina. How does that sound?"

"I come with you, you mean?"

"Why?" she says, pausing with her hands full at the dishwasher. "Did you have something else in mind?"

"Jep and I are going camping."

His mom rattles the dishes. "Is that where you were all afternoon, over at Jep's?"

"Yeah. So what?"

"What were you snacking on that ruined your appetite?"

"A couple of corn chips—Jesus, *so what?*"

"Was Jep's mother there?"

"No, Why?"

"I think it's a shame that she never seems to be home."

"She *works.*"

"So do I."

"Yeah, but nursery schools let out early," Dave says. "She has a real job."

His mother is silent.

"You know what I mean. She manages an office—"

"You should spend some time with a roomful of three-year-olds if you think it's not a real job."

"All I meant is Jep's mother works a lot of hours. What difference does it make?"

"It means she's never there." She looks at him self-consciously. "Did you smoke this afternoon?"

"*No.*"

"Well, that's good. Your clothes smell kind of—"

"For chrissakes!" Dave gets up. "I can't stand being accused all the time!"

"I wasn't accusing," his mom says in a soft voice. "Is it wrong for me to care what you're doing? Would you prefer it if we were never here?"

Yes, he feels like saying. "I can take care of myself," he says instead.

"In a lot of ways, yes." His mother takes his plate away. "By the way, what are your plans for tonight?"

"I'm going to a party."

"Oh?" She smiles. "Who's having it?"

"This girl Mindy. I forget her last name."

His mother looks up. "Don't you know her?"

"Not really."

His mom shakes her head. "Well, maybe there's something wrong with me, but I think it's nice when you know the person whose party you're going to."

"That's not how parties *are* anymore."

"Well, I'm out of step, then. I don't approve of crashing."

"I'm *going* to the party."

"Dave—"

He doesn't answer. Instead he leaves the kitchen and goes up to his room.

"Dave?"

At the bedroom door he hesitates. Should he give her a break this time? No. Why should she tell him what to do? He's seventeen years old.

4

Alone in his room, excellent. What he does first is put the Stones on the stereo. He'd like to turn it up loud, but the sound isn't that good. Maybe he should buy great components instead of a car. And new albums to replace the ones he bought before his taste changed. He can't believe some of the stuff he used to buy and listen to. Even now he's got an Elton John poster on one wall. A present from Lisa— not his own choice, at least.

Flopping down on his bed, he looks critically around him. Yeah, he's definitely got to renovate, give the place a little class. He'll find something wild instead of the plaid bedspread. Indian one like Jep's might be good, and the walls should be purple.

His parents will think it's weird. He can picture their reaction. *Purple?* Purple's sexy. He'd better not tell them that. Should he keep all the kid stuff that's still in his room—the Little League trophies and pennants and autographs? Maybe, but the Matchbox cars will definitely have to go. What he wants is a room as interesting as Jep's.

Thumping his fist to the beat of the Stones, Dave rolls over and looks up at the bulletin board over his bed. He should take down some of the old pictures, like him in his football gear, him getting confirmed at church, him at a junior high dance. He notices a shot of his parents that he took once. Man, they looked younger then. His dad has gained weight. His mom's got more lines. She's still pretty decent-looking though. Light skin and hair, which he got from her. The big features and height he got from his dad. Not bad, his parents. Much better than most. He hates to admit it, but his mom's right about Mrs. Jepson. She's never home. His parents are more like parents should be. Twenty years from now he'll probably be like them.

Not exactly though, he hopes. He'll work hard like they do, but he wants some excitement too. He can't see himself in this rut of watching TV and spending weekends on the golf course. Dave taps on the bed to the beat of "Jumping Jack Flash." One picture on the board he'll keep for sure, the one of Susan. He examines it. Beautiful, with her hair brushed off her face. Green eyes, thin lips. Some guys like full lips—he likes hers. Animal, Jep said. A *kitten*, he'd say. *You have to come tonight,* Susan told him when she left him at school. According to Willo, she comes on to everybody like that. Hell, what does Willo know? He's just jealous of Jepson. Willo's one of those guys who used to like Susan himself.

A sound in the hall makes Dave sit up quickly. He watches as a piece of paper slips under the door.

Wise-ass Lisa. He gets up and retrieves it quietly. Opening the paper, he sees an ad for a sports car. In the front seat of a Celica GT, Lisa has drawn two caricatures labeled "Dave" and "Susan S." He wishes Lisa would kindly lay off.

Sitting down in his desk chair, he examines the ad. "Two-door, four-cylinder, manual transmission, power steering and brakes. Outperforms Charger, Camaro, and Mustang in test drives." What he'd give for a Celica. He looks at the price. Ugh.

"Dave?" Lisa is outside the door. "Did you get my work of art?"

He takes a sheet of paper and writes in big letters: JACOBY ACQUITTED IN MURDER OF SISTER. Then he slips it under the door and waits for a response.

But just as he props his feet on the desk, the phone rings and after a few seconds Lisa is calling him.

"Telephone!"

Must be Jep. Dave gets up and opens the door.

"It's Susan," Lisa whispers as he passes her in the hall.

He forces himself not to run. It's the first time she's ever called him. He picks up the receiver. "Hello?" he says. Dial tone. "Hello?"

Lisa's laughing in the hall.

"What's going on?" he yells, slamming down the receiver.

"Just a joke," Lisa says. She heads for her room. "Pam called me. We were just fooling around."

"Goddam you! That headline is coming true!" Skidding around the banister, he chases her.

Lisa shuts her door and Dave hears the key turn.

"Dave?" His mom's voice comes up from the foot of the stairs. "Dave, you have company!"

"Who?"

"Bob Willoughby."

Coming down, Dave sees Willo standing in the foyer, talking to his mom.

"Ready?" Willo asks. "Jep and Susan are in the car. We're a little early, but I didn't think you'd mind. What do you say?"

Dave glances at his mother. "Is it okay if I go out?"

"Yes, go on," she says with a sigh.

"See you around, Mrs. Jacoby!"

As Willo takes off, Dave looks at his mother. "Thanks," he says quickly. "Sorry about before."

"When will we see you again?" she asks, her expression softening.

"Don't worry. No, *really*. I won't be too late."

5

"Which house is it?" Willo slows down.

"Where those cars are parked," Jep says.

Dave can't see out very well. In the front, beside Willo, are Tom and his girl friend Sandy. In the back, on Dave's left, is Bull Curtis, built like a truck. On his right Jepson sits, with Susan on Jep's lap. Susan's knees are pressing against Dave's. He can smell her clean hair.

"Turn the radio down!" Willo shouts. "Is that it?"

"Yeah."

"Man," Willo says, "her old man must be loaded."

Susan pokes him. "Sexist! Maybe her *mother's* loaded!"

"Whichever." Willo parks the car. "Looks like a great house for a bash. Who's gonna be here?"

"Kids from her school and ours."

Dave, carrying beer, trails Jep and Susan up the walk. He can hear the thump of the stereo. The doorbell chimes a tune. What a layout, Dave thinks. He waits up for Willo. "Do you know this kid Mindy?"

Willo shakes his head.

"Guess we soon will," Dave says.

Willo hoists up his six-packs. "I hear she's got a slate-topped pool table that weighs eight hundred pounds. Want to play me?"

"Maybe."

The door opens. Dave watches as Jep lifts Susan over the threshold.

"Hey, you guys *came!*" Mindy throws her arms around Jep and Susan. Susan, sliding to her feet, hugs Mindy back.

Jep grins. "We brought a few friends along."

"Terrific!" Mindy says. "And you brought more beer? Excellent. Come on down to the rec room."

Dave nods at Mindy. "Hi."

"Hi! The more the merrier, right? This person I know had a party fifty people crashed. I told her, 'I'm gonna top that!' Come on downstairs."

Dave walks behind Mindy. Definitely not his type. Too much makeup, clothes too flashy. In those big balloony pants she could pass for Humpty Dumpty.

Downstairs music blares. Dave looks around the room. Kids, slouched on the sofa and sprawled on the floor, are drinking but they don't seem to be having that good a time. He doesn't recognize them—they must be from Mindy's school.

Willo tugs Dave's arm. "Hey, *some* pool table, Jacoby. What do you say, a little stripes and solids?"

"Later," Dave says, taking in the furniture and fancy tiled floor. Pinball, Atari, Betamax—nothing spared.

"Jacoby?" Willo, nudging him, points to a door. "Know what's behind there? Mindy just told me. A hot tub, I swear."

"No kidding?" As Dave turns he sees somebody he knows. Nan from California, with her hair loose for a change. Usually she puts it down the middle of her back in a braid like a rope.

"Want to play one of the video games?" Willo asks Dave.

"Not now," Dave says. Leaning against the wall, he decides he hates the beginnings of parties. Everybody's so awkward, phony, and forced. He looks around for Susan and Jep.

"I got a game," Jep's telling Mindy. "It'll liven things up. It can get a little messy, but with this kind of floor it's okay."

"What is it?" Mindy asks.

"Beer Hunter."

Dave smiles. One of those games Jep makes up as he goes along.

Mindy bats her eyelashes. "How do you play it?"

Jep has an audience now. He waits until they're quiet. "You know how, in the movie *The Deer Hunter,* they play Russian roulette?"

"Yeah," Mindy says.

"Okay, Beer Hunter is Russian roulette using a six-pack instead of a gun."

"How do you mean?"

"Instead of getting shot, you risk drowning in beer." Jep lifts up a six-pack and hands the cans around. "Take one," he urges. "Here you go, Jacoby. Okay, this is the game: One of these cans I shook up, before. We're all going to open them up now. Hold your head over it. Five of us won't have any problem—open the can and enjoy drinking it. But the loser—well, you'll see—he'll get sloshed, literally." Pulling the tab on the can, Jep backs off as beer spurts in his face. The front of his shirt is drenched. Bubbles of foam cling to his mustache. As the spectators hoot at him, Susan wipes Jep's face.

Willo looks up from his beer can. "What's the point?" he asks.

Jep takes a long swallow. "Just to liven things up."

"How about pool?" Willo asks. "Doesn't anybody want to shoot pool?"

Mindy puts her arm around Jep. "No, let's play Beer Hunter."

"Okay." Jep circulates, organizing two groups.

Someone turns up the stereo, and Springsteen sings "Born to Run." Dave watches Jep rounding up kids, and when Susan offers her hand he joins in the circle. Jep passes more beer around. Susan takes her turn. She pulls the tab. "Oops!" she cries as a little bit spills out.

It's Dave's turn. He tugs hard and spray hits his face. As beer trickles down his neck, Jep pounds him on the back. Susan dabs his chin with the sleeve of her shirt. "Poor Dave," she laughs.

Dave lets more beer trickle over him. Good, she's wiping his chin again. Meanwhile the other circle is getting pretty raucous. Bull Curtis spills beer. Fresh six-packs are passed around and the noise level increases. The telephone rings, but Mindy doesn't hear it. Cans clatter to the floor and new crashers arrive. Jep, with one arm around Susan and one around Dave, sings along with Springsteen. "Party's starting to liven up."

"Yeah," Dave agrees. "How'd you think up this game?"

"I'm just a genius, I guess. Hey, are we working on the *Carrion* tomorrow?"

"Sure," Dave says. "Whenever you say."

"Not too early." Jep hugs Susan. "This may be a long night."

Another round follows another. Dave loses track of time. He's aware all of a sudden that the noise has died down, and he's sitting on the floor, more or less by himself. Jep and Susan are on the couch now, whispering to each other. As Dave watches, they get up and walk across the room. At one point he thinks that they're motioning for him to come, but he decides that they aren't. They go off by themselves to the room where the hot tub is.

Dave sits for a little while, eyes on the closed door. Getting up, he roams restlessly around. Willo's involved in a game of pool by this time. Tom and Sandy, on the couch, are so tangled up he can't tell one of them from the other. Hanging on to a can of beer, Dave tries not to look lost. Suddenly he feels crummy. The smell of beer is making him sick. Mindy's laugh, drifting across the room, makes him feel even sicker. He'd like to go home, but he doesn't want to walk four miles. Willo isn't about to leave, so if he goes, he's on his own. Only thing to do is to hitchhike from the highway. Dave heads across the room to look for his jacket.

"Hi," Nan says unexpectedly. She's standing at the bottom of the stairs.

He turns. "Hi. I was just—" He pauses, unwilling to sound like he's avoiding her. "I was going for a beer. Want one?"

"No thanks."

"Guess I'll skip it then, too."

"I didn't expect to know anyone here," Nan says. "Are you friends with Mindy?"

"No," Dave says. "Just chance. I came with Susan and Jep."

"Where are they?" Nan asks. "Did they leave?"

"I don't think so." Dave stares at the redwood door. *What are they doing in there?* "How do you know Mindy?" he asks. Some conversation.

"She's my second cousin," Nan says, "but we don't know each other well. It's just that she's my only relative around here and she feels as if she ought to befriend me or something."

Dave nods. The silence is awkward. "So how do you like New York by now? The New York suburbs, I mean." He feels like a quiz show host. As soon as she answers he'll excuse himself quick.

"Belle Park seems like a good place, but I haven't been here long enough—" Nan, glancing up hesitantly, goes on in a rush. "It happened unexpectedly. I thought I was all set in Santa Barbara, and then my father's company decided to send him here."

"That's rough." Dave looks at Nan more closely. Her lips pucker up when she says certain words. She's rounder than Susan—not heavy, just rounder. He clears his throat. "So your whole family came here?"

"Just my father and me. My parents are divorced."

"Yeah? That must be rough." Is *rough* all he can say? "Where's your mother?"

"In California."

"Oh." There's something kind of nice about Nan's low voice, he thinks.

"I lived with her the last two years," Nan says. "Now it's my father's turn."

"Turn?"

"They share custody."

"That's how you like it?"

Nan shrugs. "The way I like it, it can't be."

"Living with both of them, you mean."

Nan nods. "They both said I could stay in California with my mother, but I know how my father was counting on this." Her eyes wander. "It's been four years they're divorced. You'd think by now I'd be used to it."

"But you aren't."

"Right." Nan's eyes meet his. "Are your parents divorced?"

"No, they're together." He smiles. "Very together and both on my back."

"You don't sound like you mind too much."

"It depends on what mood I'm in. Tonight at dinner I got annoyed. They were giving me a hard time."

Nan is quiet for a moment. Then she looks at him cautiously. "Are you having a good time?"

"Here? Yeah, I guess. How about you?"

"This minute, yes, but before, I felt *detached*. I felt like an onlooker. And then I noticed you, and I thought maybe you felt it, too. I guess I was wrong," she says, smiling to herself. "My best friend Jane in California used to tell me I analyzed too much."

Dave squeezes his empty beer can. "No, you're right," he says slowly. "I *was* feeling detached. I was watching, not enjoying myself. Pretty depressing, huh?"

"Not really," Nan says. "I wouldn't want to be an onlooker all the time, but sometimes it's kind of interesting, like watching a movie. Since I came here I've had a lot of chances to be an observer, and I'm learning a lot." She smiles again, this time at Dave.

"What are you learning?" She's all right, he decides. Long lashes, brown eyes, a really nice mouth.

"Oh, it sounds stupid to say it because it's all pretty obvious, but basically—that most people are just trying to impress each other."

Dave nods. "I guess you're right. I *know* you're right. Hell, I'm one of them."

"One of who?"

"One of the people who are trying to impress."

"You are?" Nan's lips pucker and she laughs. "You shouldn't have told me. I thought you *were* impressive. You mean it's all a big act?"

"Yeah. Maybe I'm not one of the worst types you're thinking of, but I'm that way sometimes."

"What way?" she asks. Someone bumps into her now and she edges under the stairs.

"How do I try to impress people?" Dave moves along with her. "Oh, I try to act cool. I like people to think I'm—"

"Macho?"

"I guess. It's not like I'm so physical or I want to be tough or anything. It's just that I don't want people thinking I'm boring."

Nan shakes her head. "You aren't. Look, I hardly know you at all, but the very fact that you think about this stuff means you can't be that bad off. The kind of phonies I'm talking about have no idea what they're doing."

Dave toys with his beer can. "Well, I hope you're right. Once in a while, though, I have these urges to show off. I picture myself doing something that makes everybody turn around."

"I have fantasies like that, too," Nan says. "Don't think only men have them."

"What are yours?" he asks.

Her lips pucker again. "I used to dream of winning a marathon. I still jog now, but not seriously. I picture myself writing a best-seller sometimes."

"Is that what you're working on when I see you in health class?"

"No." She smiles. "That's just fooling around."

Dave moves farther under the stairs as he's jostled from

the rear. "All I know is your printing is incredibly neat."

"Thanks."

"I wish mine was. I've got this thing I have to do." Dave pauses. "You wouldn't be interested in helping by any chance?"

"Printing? I can type, too. What is it, a term paper?"

"No, an April Fool's parody. It should turn out pretty good. Jep and I are working on it. Would you be willing to—?"

"Type it? Sure."

"Great," Dave says. "I could bring it to you when we finish tomorrow. Where do you live?"

"Hampton Place."

"Oh, yeah, yeah. I know—that little street in the woods. Is your phone number listed?"

"Yes."

"I'll give you a ring then." Dave glances around as Bull Curtis approaches him. "What's up?"

Curtis thumps him on the arm. "You're wanted, Jacoby."

"By who?"

"Susan."

Dave steps out from under the stairs.

"She needs help with Jepson. He's bombed."

"Again?"

"Go look for yourself."

"Where?"

"In the hot tub. He drank gin and he almost passed out."

Dave sees that the door to the hot tub room is open. "Excuse me," he says, barely looking at Nan.

Someone's blocking the doorway.

"Let Dave in!" Susan calls.

Dave goes inside and quickly shuts the door.

"Dave, thank God! This is awful!" Susan's holding Jep by the wrists. Jep's submerged up to his neck. His head bounces against the rim of the tub. "Come on in, man," he mumbles.

Dave can't help smiling at Jep's serene face. "Some other time," he tells him. "How'd you get like this?"

Jep grins back at him. Susan tugs at Jep's wrists. "Come on. This is stupid! People can drown in these things!"

Dave, taking over, keeps Jep from slipping down further. "Where'd he get the gin?"

"He brought it with him," Susan says. "You know that book we're doing in English by F. Scott Fitzgerald?"

"Yeah?"

"Jep read that Fitzgerald and his wife once got drunk and jumped in a fountain."

"This is his version?"

"Yes," Susan says. "It was funny at first. Jep!" she calls. "Help Dave get you out."

Jep, smiling, stands up in his dripping jockey shorts and lets Dave pull him out of the tub. "Think I'm disgusting?" Jep asks as Dave dries him off.

"No comment."

Jep smiles and sways. Susan, glaring, looks at the puddle on the floor. "He always goes too far. Why does he have to do that?"

"Easy, man." Dave helps Jep pull his jeans over his wet shorts. "Now what?"

"We'll have to get him home," Susan says. "Can you believe this? He's messed up the rest of the evening. See if Willo can take him home."

"Sit here for a second," Dave says to Jep. While Jep sits on the edge of the tub, Dave goes over to the pool table. "We got a problem," he says to Willo. "Do you think you could take Jep home?"

Willo digs for his keys. "I'm in the middle of this now. You take him. You can keep my car. I'll get a ride later and pick it up in front of your house."

"Thanks." Dave slaps palms with Willo and goes back to where Susan is holding Jep up. Humming to himself now, Jep lets Dave take over. "I'm driving you both home," Dave says. "Willo's lending me the car."

"Can we come back?" Susan asks.

"No, forget it. It's getting late."

"What a bore," Susan moans, following Dave and Jep up the stairs.

Dave looks around for Nan, but he doesn't see her anywhere.

Mindy notices them coming up and walks to the door. "He's such a fun guy," she says, beaming at Jep. "I'm sorry you have to go."

"I'm sorry too." Susan rolls her eyes.

Mindy hugs her. "Glad you came though. Take good care of him!"

Dave lugs Jep to the car, helps get him settled on the back seat, and then leans over to unlock the door for Susan from the inside. Sliding behind the wheel, he can hear Jep snoring as Susan gets in and rests her head on the seat back. Dave clears his throat. "Should I take you home first?"

Susan smiles at him strangely. "No, don't do that. Take Jep home first."

6

Warming up Willo's car, Dave tries to get a look at Susan. In the dim light all he sees is a dark silhouette. For a moment as he pulls away he thinks she might have fallen asleep too. Good, it'll make things less complicated.

Driving along, he fiddles with the radio until he finds a commercial-free station. When he slows for the first light, he can't help being curious. "Susan?" he says.

"Yes?"

"You awake?" Brilliant question.

"Yeah, I am. Do me a favor?"

"What?"

"Fasten my seat belt."

"You serious? Okay." His arm brushes against her as he reaches for the buckle. He's imagined a scene like this. It's one of his best fantasies. Now it's real. As his hand lightly touches her arm, she shifts. Shoving the buckle into the slot, he keeps his hand there.

"Thanks," Susan whispers.

Dave reluctantly takes his hand away. "You're welcome." He steps on the gas. Damn, he can't remember where he's going. Jep's house, and take it easy—don't make too much of this. She still goes with Jep. Nothing has changed. Shifting gears, Dave turns left. "Is Jepson okay back there?"

"Feeling no pain," Susan says. "What did you think of the party?"

"Okay, I guess. . . ."

Susan sighs. "It would have been if Jep hadn't passed out. How do you like Mindy's house?"

Dave smiles. "Something else."

"And Mindy?"

Dave stops for a light. "Nice, but not my type."

"No? Who *is* your type?"

He can see her face now. "Well—"

"That girl from school you were talking to?"

"Who, Nan Tobin?" He shakes his head.

"Come on," Susan urges. "Tell me who your type is."

"I can't—"

Susan jostles his arm. "You're so cute when you're shy. I bet your face is red."

"No, it's not." Dave smiles.

Susan leans toward him as far as the seat belt allows. "I like the way you drive," she says.

"Yeah? How?"

"With this serious expression, like you're flying a mission." She laughs.

"You're mocking me out."

"No, no, it's cute!"

Usually he can't stand that word. In this case he keeps smiling.

Susan leans toward him again. "Jep says you two are getting a car."

"We're thinking about it."

"That's neat. What kind?"

"An Audi 5000."

"What's that?"

Dave turns onto Harrison Street. "Just kidding. That's what my parents would probably buy if they had the dough. Jep and I will have to get something much more routine."

"I think convertibles are excellent," Susan says. "Mindy's brother has a VW Rabbit."

"They're nice, but still too expensive for us."

Susan wrinkles her nose. "Do me a favor, don't buy an old car that smells like this one does."

"I'll try not to."

Susan's face catches light from the street. "By the way, where is Jep getting the money to put into a car?"

"I'm lending it to him."

"You are? That's really nice of you." She pauses. "You're so—*good.*"

"I don't know how to take that," he says. "Sounds like you mean I shouldn't be."

She laughs. "Dave, you're sweet. I like you just the way you are."

Too soon they're in front of Jep's building. "Here we are," Dave says. "Jep, wake up!" Reaching behind him, Dave grabs his leg. "Rise and shine, man. Come on, look alive!"

Jep mutters. One of his legs twitches.

Dave gets out of the car. "Jepson?" He shakes him again.

"Lemme alone!"

Dave tugs at Jep's dead weight, but he can't get him to move. "Now what?" he asks Susan.

"This is ridiculous," she says. "Take me home, I guess."

Damn it, he thinks. What was he hoping for, anyway? Crawling behind the wheel again, he starts up the car.

Susan rolls her window down and a rush of cool air blows in. Her hair fans out on the seat so that Dave can smell her lemon-scented shampoo. "How fast can this car go?" she asks as they round a curve.

"Oh, seventy-five at least on the open road," Dave says. "In town here, hell, the cops would be on me at fifty."

Susan locks her hands together. "I can't wait till you guys get your own car. When do you think it'll be?"

"Soon, I hope."

"Turn at the next corner!"

"I know," he says. He's known exactly where she lives since at least seventh grade. Stopping at the curb, Dave glances at the back seat. "Any life there?"

"Save your breath," Susan says. "He gives me a pain."

"Yeah, well—" Dave notices Susan reaching for her safety belt. "Want me to get it?" he asks.

"Sure."

He opens the buckle. "You're free," he says. He wishes.

"Jep!" Susan calls out. "If you don't wake up now, tough luck. I'm warning you."

Dave, hearing Jep snore, looks over at Susan.

Susan opens the door, but she doesn't get out. "Thank God you're awake, anyway," she says in a low voice. Leaning toward him, she kisses him and slips quickly out of the car.

"Susan?" he calls, but she's already halfway down the path. "*Susan?*" He sees her going into her house. Touching his mouth, he still can't believe it. He considers going after her, but in the back seat Jep moans.

Dave sits up guilty. "What's the matter?"

Jep coughs. "Don't feel so good."

"Hang in, okay?" Dave backs the car around.

Jep moans again.

"Hey, what's wrong?"

"I'm gonna be sick!"

"Should I stop?" Dave accelerates. He turns into Jep's street.

"Hurry," Jep urges.

"Hold on, we're here."

Jep throws the door open.

"Wait a second!" Dave calls.

But Jep lurches out and hangs his head over the gutter. Dave, at his side, holds him as Jep starts to heave.

"Oh, God," Jep moans after the first noisy gush.

Dave hangs onto his waist. "Go ahead—again."

Jep leans over, supported by Dave, until the retching finally stops.

Dave digs into his pocket for a wadded-up tissue.

"Whew." Jep wipes his mouth. "What a hell of a mess."

"Finished?"

"Yeah, poor you. Look at your shoes."

"Forget it," Dave says, helping him up. "How are you doing?"

Jep leans on him. "Pukey. What happened to Susan?"

"I took her home just now."

"You took her?"

"*We* did."

"We did? Thanks a lot." Jep hiccups. "Don't tell her about this."

Dave nods. "Don't worry, I won't."

Jep leans on Dave's arm as they go into his building. "Susan's mad at me, I guess. Did she say she was mad?"

"Yeah."

"I didn't think I was getting that polluted. I'll have to make it up to her . . . don't want her to be mad."

Dave silently pushes the elevator button.

"Want to come up?" Jep asks.

"No, thanks, I've got to get home."

The elevator comes. Jep gets in and presses the hold button. "How about it? Just for a couple of minutes."

"I can't," Dave says.

Jep keeps holding the button. "Man, what a night. *Women,* I swear. You know what I can't wait for?"

Dave backs away from the elevator. "What?"

"For that trip out to Montauk. No women—just us."

"Me too," Dave says. "Hey, can you make it upstairs?"

Jep sways, then straightens up. "Are you kidding? Why couldn't I?" To prove it, he lets go of the button and the elevator goes up.

Returning to Willo's Chevy, Dave gets in and drives home. On the way he touches his lips, which feel tingling and strange. He keeps thinking about Susan as he parks Willo's car. When he reaches the back door, he takes off his messy shoes and, holding them under the outdoor faucet, washes them off. Inside, the house is quiet. He sees by the kitchen clock that it's just after one. Carrying the dripping shoes in front of him, he goes up the stairs.

"Dave?"

"Yeah?"

"You're in for the night?" His mom appears in her bathrobe.

"Yeah," he says, quickly hiding the shoes behind his back.

"Good night."

"Night." He goes into his room, turns on the light, and on his pillow sees another message from Lisa. "Sorry I was mean before," she has written in the margin of a newspaper. "Here are some cars maybe you can afford."

His eyes run down the column of classified aids. BUICK LE SABRE, $1900. CHEVY MALIBU, $2100. He sees the heading FOREIGN/SPORTS CARS and pauses on one item.

VW BUG, FULL CANVAS SUNRF. RUNS EXCEL.
LOOKS SHARP. $795. 458–6734.

Sunroof—a convertible, almost, and the price makes it possible. Still thinking of Susan, Dave takes off his clothes and crawls into bed. Dammit, what can he do to keep from driving himself nuts over her? Put his mind on the car. That's the only way out. First thing in the morning he'll go take a look at it. It's about time he did something big on his own.

7

Dave shifts gears and pulls away from the curb. The VW bug makes a *putt-putt*ing sound. He smiles at Keith, the guy who's selling the car. Keith, on the sidewalk, waves him right on.

Nice dude, to let him take it out and try it on his own. Dave slips into high gear and chugs down Nassau Avenue. The newspaper ad was right—the car definitely looks sharp. Keith's friend who works in a body shop gave it a great paint job. Dave loves the way the silver reflects the morning sun. Stopping at the first light, he examines the interior again.

The inside could be a little sharper, but he can't be too fussy. After all, the car is fourteen years old. He could probably tape the places where the seat cover is torn. And because of the sunroof, the car doesn't smell bad. It's got a few extras—a heater, a radio. He rolls back the canvas sunroof and breathes in fresh air.

Dave accelerates. He loves the sound. It reminds him of the power mower he used to use when he was a kid to make money cutting grass. Turning onto Belle Park Avenue, he sees a station wagon something like his father's. His parents must be wondering where the hell he went. He'll call them up later.

Now he turns onto Dixon. Seems like some things you can't control. It's Susan's street, and one of his dreams last night suddenly comes back to him. He feels weak again just thinking about it. Driving slowly, he has a fantasy: Susan will come out and tell him that Jep wants to break up. Shifting into low, Dave passes Susan's house. He stares up at her window, but she's nowhere in sight. Actually what he should be doing is having Jep see the car. Making a U-turn, he heads toward Franklin Street and Jep's.

Idling in front of Jep's building, Dave beeps out the same tattoo on the horn that Willo always uses as a signal. Nothing. No reaction. Jep must be sleeping off his hangover. Dave honks one more time, but when the superintendent looks out, he decides to drive off and get Jep to go over to Keith's later. Backtracking to Nassau, Dave pictures how it'll be from now on: no more begging rides or bumping along on Jep's Moped. As he turns onto Keith's block, the knob on the stick shift falls off. Damn, he'd better go over the car carefully for little things like that.

Dave sees Keith waiting for him when he pulls up in front of his house. The guy looks very 1960's, with a ponytail and scruffy jeans. Keith claims he's twenty-eight, but he looks a lot younger. He opens the door on the side opposite Dave. "What do you think?"

"I like it a lot. Nice."

"Want to buy it?" Keith asks.

"This knob just fell off." Dave gropes for it under the seat.

Keith finds it. "No problem. A little epoxy."

Dave leans back. "How come you're selling it?"

"I'm going to Dallas next week. I'm getting a new car down there."

"How long have you had it?"

Keith slides in next to Dave. "Three years. I bought it from the original owner. You know cars? You work on cars?"

"Not much." Dave clears his throat. "I will soon, though. I'm learning."

Keith puts the knob temporarily back on the stick. "Yeah, well, I've kept this up pretty good. I did a lot of the repairs myself."

There's a moment of silence. "So what do you think?" Keith repeats.

"I think I'll bring my friend and my dad over this afternoon."

"Fine," Keith says. "Just one thing I think I'd better tell you in fairness. I got a few calls while you were out on the road. One was this friend who knows the car already. He wants it. I told him, 'Another guy's here—he gets first crack.'"

Dave looks at him. "This guy definitely wants it?"

"Yeah, if you don't. Sorry to pressure you—"

"I was figuring on more time."

Keith nods sympathetically. "Yeah, well, whoever comes up with the money first."

"This guy has the money?"

"He can get it—all cash. How about you?" Keith asks. "You've got it on you?"

"Hell, no," Dave says. "I'd have to go to the bank. They're open till noon today."

Keith sighs. "Saturday's a bummer. Motor Vehicles is closed. Look, do you want the car for sure?"

Dave wets his lips. "I've got to tell you now?"

"Yeah, I have to settle. I'm leaving on Tuesday. How about this?" Keith tosses his ponytail. "Bring half the money as a deposit now. That way I'll hold the car for you. You'll take possession Monday, when we transfer the plates. On Monday I'll drive you over there—"

"I go to school Monday," Dave says.

"Could you cut out a little early?"

"I guess so."

"One o'clock?"

Dave is silent for a moment. "This friend of yours," he says suspiciously, "you're sure you aren't hyping me?"

Keith lets out a sigh. "I could sell this car ten times over, man. If you aren't sure, don't buy it."

"I want it," Dave says.

"Good. Drive it to the bank. See how I trust you? The registration's in there." Keith tugs, but the glove compartment sticks. "No problem," he says. "A little oil, that's all."

Dave grips the wheel as Keith gets out and shuts the door.

"See you later," Keith says.

"Yeah." Dave drives down the street. He can't believe what he's doing. The thought crosses his mind—what if Jep hates this car? So what? He'll buy it by himself regardless, he decides suddenly.

Jep is lounging on his bed late in the afternoon. "Okay, here's the last one: BELLE PARK MAJORETTES STAR IN PORNO FILM."

Dave forces a smile.

"What's the matter?" Jep asks.

"Nothing." Dave looks away. It's just hitting him full force. He felt so sure a couple of hours ago. Now he's wondering, was he ripped off?

"Jacoby!"

"What?"

"Did you hear what I said?"

"Yeah, yeah, go on." Dave makes notes, but he can't concentrate, with four hundred bucks paid down and the rest in his wallet.

"Put all the names of the majorettes in the article," Jep says. "They'll love seeing their names. That's what'll make the paper sell."

Dave scribbles distractedly. He should tell Jep he bought the car. No. Now that he's gone this far, he'll make it a surprise.

Jep, leaning back, scratches his bare feet. "Who did you say was typing this up for us?"

Dave snaps to attention. "Nan Tobin said she'd do it."

"That kid from health class? You'd better take it to her now. My mom's secretary needs it Monday."

Dave nods. "I'll walk over there now, I guess."

"Take my Moped." Jep picks up his guitar. "What are you doing tonight? Want to come back and jam?"

"Okay. I'll go home and eat and pick up my bass."

Jep strikes a chord. "What did you do today, sleep?"

"No, I went out." Dave shields his eyes.

"See anybody?"

"No."

"Speak to Susan?" Jep asks.

"No. Why?"

"I just wondered if she's still mad at me. I called but she was out." Jep strums with the pick. "I hope she's not off me for good over this."

Dave gets up from the mattress. "I'll try calling Nan." Ducking under the netting, he goes to the phone. "Nan? This is Dave Jacoby. Can I bring over the typing? Good. Which house again? Okay. See you—good-bye."

He hangs up the receiver and starts back to Jep's bedroom. This is dumb. He's going to tell Jep about Susan kissing him and about the car. If you can't tell your best friend, who the hell *can* you tell? "Jep?" he calls out, but Jep isn't in the room.

"Take the key to the Moped," Jep shouts from the bathroom. "It's there on the bureau. And hurry back, man. Make like you're driving a Jaguar XJS. And don't do anything I wouldn't do over at Nan's house!"

8

Dave bumps along Franklin Street on Jep's beat-up Moped, the pages for Nan tucked in his belt. He wishes he could relax about getting the car on Monday, but instead he's convinced that something is going to go wrong. Keith could take off, for instance, with the car and half the money. For the tenth time Dave checks the wallet in his pocket. All he needs is to lose his other six hundred bucks.

"Dave?"

He turns his head.

"Dave!"

He almost tips over.

"Hi!" Susan waves from the island in the middle of the street.

He stops at the curb, so that horns begin to honk.

Susan, swinging a shopping bag, snakes her way around the stopped cars. "Can I have a ride?" she calls.

"Yeah, hop on. Hurry up."

The bag dangling from her arm, she clasps Dave around the waist.

He takes off. Horns honk again.

Susan clings to him tightly. "Where are you going?"

He can barely hear her voice. "I'm delivering something. How about you?"

"Home. Can you take me first?"

"Yeah." He makes a turn. Then he weaves in and out, all the time thinking of the kiss in the car last night. He can't decide what to say so he doesn't say anything.

Finally Susan leans forward and presses her head against him. "What did you do today?" she asks.

"Looked at cars," he says.

"You did? Great! What did you see?"

He stops at a traffic light. "I saw this VW."

"A Rabbit?"

"No." He starts up again. "A real nice old beetle."

"What color?"

"Silver."

"What else did you see?"

"That's about it."

As the Moped goes over a manhole cover, Susan hooks her thumbs in his belt loops. "Next time you go looking, can I come along with you?"

Should he tell her it's already his? No. "Yeah, you can come with me."

"Good. I love to shop. I bought a sweater. Want to see it?"

"Now?"

She squeezes him. "No, David, when we get *home* I'll show it to you!"

David, he likes that. He steers over a bump.

Susan laughs. "Dave, be careful! Turn—you know, my street is next."

He takes a left and slows down to make the ride last. Now traffic is behind them. They're on Dixon, near her house. He zigzags a little, just to show off.

"Dave, stop!" she calls out, but she laughs again as she

says it. "You're getting crazy, I swear, as crazy as Jep!"

He pulls up at her house.

"Thanks," she says warmly. Sliding off the bike, she takes the sweater out of the bag. "See?" she says. "Like it?"

Dave nods. "Yeah, you look good in pink."

"Do you think so?" She keeps watching him as she puts the sweater back in the bag. "What are you doing later on tonight?"

"I told Jep I'd go back there," Dave says uncertainly.

"Oh. Too bad. I would have asked you over. How *is* Jep?" she asks.

"He's okay. He called you this afternoon."

"I know. I was here, but I told my mother to say I wasn't." Susan's eyes are on him. "You think that's mean, don't you? You don't believe in doing things like that."

"No, well . . ." Dave shrugs.

Susan looks at him quickly. "Can I tell you something private?"

"Yeah, sure."

"I don't know if I want to go with Jep anymore."

"No?" Dave feels his neck and his ears getting warm.

"I've been thinking about it," Susan says, rustling her shopping bag. "It's not just last night. . . . I've outgrown him, I think. I used to love how he was always the mover at parties. Now I feel it's so childish. Don't you think it is?"

Dave shrugs again.

"I should tell him, I guess, but I can't stand hurting him." Susan casts her eyes upward. "Please don't *you* tell him. He'd be very upset."

"Yeah, he would."

"I still *like* him," Susan says, "but it has to be more than that. It's so hard, telling somebody your feelings have changed." Susan brushes back her hair. "We've been going together it'll be a year in June. He's already talking about our first anniversary. I wish, oh—" Her voice breaks. "Never mind. Forget it. I'd better go in. . . ."

He moves a step toward her, but she hurries up the path. "Thanks for the ride," she calls over her shoulder. "And please don't tell Jep."

"I won't."

"Can we go to look at cars on Monday after school?" she shouts from the front step.

Dave is silent for a second. "I guess so," he says.

"Great. See you then!" Susan goes into the house.

Dave, back on the Moped, can barely read the street signs. The sun is down. Damn, he's going to be late for dinner again. Jep expects him back. Nan's waiting, too. Here's her house, finally. He turns into the cul-de-sac and parks the Moped.

Nan opens the door. "Hi. Come on in. Did you get lost?"

"No, sidetracked a little." Stepping inside, he looks at the small-paneled windows, peaked ceiling, and beams. "Hey, this is a neat house."

"Yes, it's pretty quaint," Nan says. "Early Snow White and the Seven Dwarves. Little animals come in every day and help me sweep up."

Dave, smiling, follows her into the living room. "Where are they now?"

"They get weekends off."

"Not like poor you, right? We've got you working over-time." He pulls the papers out from his belt.

Nan takes them. "I'll charge you extra."

Dave shoves his hands into his pockets. "Can you read my lousy writing?"

"Yeah." Nan scans the headlines of the *Carrion*. "This is good." She laughs. "You did this whole thing?"

"Jep and I. You know Jepson—famous voice on the P.A.?"

"I don't really know him, but I feel like I do." Nan looks over the articles. "I love things like this. My friend Jane and I used to try to write satire."

"If we'd known, you could have helped us. We were straining by the end." Dave glances around the room. Big fireplace, lots of books. A picture of Nan as a kid with her mom and dad.

Nan laughs again as she turns the page. Then she looks up. "I'm really a great hostess. Would you like to sit down?"

"For a second," he says.

She leads him to the couch.

"Think you'll have time to finish typing by tomorrow night?" he asks.

"Sure. I'll call you as soon as I'm done." Sitting down next to him, she drops the papers into her lap. "How did things work out last night? Was Jep okay eventually?"

"After he threw up."

"You took him home?"

"Yeah. Sorry I disappeared on you like that—I looked for you before I left."

"You did? Thanks. I left early, too," Nan says. "Does Jep do that often?"

"Not really. He's not an alcoholic or anything." Dave leans forward, hands on his knees. "Some people think he's childish, but I kind of envy him. He does everything to the maximum." Dave smiles to himself.

"What are you smiling at?"

"I was thinking of this thing he did a couple of months ago. He told this girl at a disco that he was twenty-three years old."

"Did she believe him?"

"Until she saw the high school I.D. in his wallet." Dave chuckles. "He made up an excuse, but the magic was gone for her."

"He goes with Susan Scherra, doesn't he?" Nan asks.

"Yeah." Dave clears his throat. "Do you know her?"

"Only from classes. She's beautiful."

Dave nods. "She's—never mind."

Nan watches him in silence. "So how's Jep feeling today?"

"Okay. He's better."

"And how about you?"

"Me? I wasn't drinking that much. I'm okay."

"You don't look too sure." She smiles. "What did you do today?"

"Bought a car." How come he's telling *her?*

"Really? That's great!"

"I hope so. We'll see."

Nan looks at him, puzzled. "Why? Is something wrong?"

"I'm supposed to get it Monday, if the guy hasn't skipped town."

"Why, who did you buy it from?"

"Some guy who wanted cash, who's leaving for Dallas. I should have insisted on giving him a check."

"Where's the car now?" Nan asks.

"At his house—it better be. I have a receipt," Dave says, "but I'm still kind of spooked." He reaches into his pocket.

Nan examines the paper. "It looks okay to me. If you're worried about him, why don't you call?"

"And say what, 'Oh, you're there? Great! I thought you skipped town'?"

"Just see if he is. If he is, you'll feel better." Nan nudges him. "Go on, there's the phone over there."

Dave gets up reluctantly. "Nothing to fear but fear itself, right?" He takes out the number, then he dials and the phone rings. Dave looks at Nan. On the fourth ring he hears Keith say hello.

"Hi—Dave Jacoby," he says, "the guy who bought your car today? I just wanted to make sure what time you said on Monday—one o'clock? Good. Thanks a lot. Sorry to bother you. So long." Hanging up, he smiles at Nan and raises both fists over his head. "You were right. I was being paranoid. It's a good thing you told me to call."

9

Oh, what a feeling! like they say in those car ads. Heading toward the school on Harrison, he shifts into high gear. As of this hour the car is all his. It's paid for, insured, with license number 1440-BAT. Keith even repaired a couple of things. Pushing back the sunroof, Dave takes a deep breath. Now for the best part—showing it off.

Jep and Susan will both be wondering where he disappeared to. Susan still thinks they're going to shop for cars today. He wishes she'd hurry up and tell Jep that her feelings have changed. Makes him feel so damned crummy to know something that Jep doesn't know. Dave starts to slow down as he approaches the school zone. He's been thinking about Susan more and more, though he's trying hard not to. He's early, he notices—classes aren't out yet. Looking around for a space, he sees Jep standing in the parking lot. "Jepson! What are you doing out there?" Dave calls out the window.

Jep jumps off his Moped. "Jacoby! Whose wheels are those?"

Dave drapes one arm out the window. "Mine."

"Yours?"

It's been worth all the worry to see Jepson's face right now. "I bought it on Saturday," Dave says. "I decided to buy it myself."

Jep, grinning, points a finger at him. "Yours? You're not bulling me?"

Dave nods.

"You sly bastard! Yahoo!" Jep shouts. He thumps on the hood. "I *thought* something was going on." He flings the door open. "Hey, it's for real." He shakes his head in disbelief. "You *surprised* me. Congratulations, man." He slaps Dave's palm as he gets into the car. "Silver. I *like* it." Jep eyes the tape on the seats. "Not bad—a good match. A radio? Terrific. Sunroof, ashtray ... Where'd you get it, anyway?"

"Off this guy over on Nassau. He gave me a good deal."

"How much?"

"Seven ninety-five."

"Not bad. How old is it?"

"Fourteen."

"Hell, *young.* Still going through puberty. How does the motor sound?"

"Great. Like a souped-up Lawn-Boy."

Jep smiles. "What do you think it'll do?"

"Seventy, if I pushed it."

"I'm floored, man." Jep slaps the seat.

"Glad you like it," Dave says. "You can borrow it whenever."

"Thanks. How about tomorrow?" Jep slouches. "I've got time on my hands."

"How come?"

He clamps his knees together. "I'm suspended for three days."

"So that's why you're out here. What was it, the asbestos thing?"

Jep nods. "It must have hit Schultz that I was the only

guy missing from class. Richards called me in a couple of periods ago. He wasn't amused."

"Should you be hanging around here?"

"Hell, no. I should be off the school grounds. I was waiting for Susan. What's eating her, anyway?"

Dave shifts. "Why, what makes you think—?"

"She's acting so bad! Hell, I apologized for the party." Jep toys with his mustache. "She's got *homework,* she says. She can't see me today. When I told her I'm suspended, I swear she was glad." Jep glances at Dave. "What do you think is going on?"

"Ask *her,*" Dave says evenly.

"I did. She won't tell me." Jep thinks for a second. "Maybe I ought to romance her a little bit. Take her some place in your car . . . some place like the beach."

"You'll freeze your tails off," Dave says. "It's March 31."

"God." Jep claps his hand to his head. "April Fool's Day's tomorrow. I won't be in school for selling the *Carrion.* You'll have to take care of the whole thing."

"Don't worry. I'll get help."

Jep pounds his head with his fist. "It kills me, I can't tell you! Seeing everybody's reaction is the best part!" He tips his head back. "Can I borrow the car at least?"

"Tomorrow? I—guess so."

"Good. I'll take Susan to the beach during school."

"Hey, wait, she's one of the people who could help me sell the *Carrion!*" Dave watches as kids come out of the building. "Speaking of the devil," he says, "here she comes."

Jep peers out. "Who's that she's with?"

"Bull Curtis and Mazur."

Jep glances at him. "Think one of them could be fooling around with her?"

"No," Dave says loudly.

Bull leaves and Susan walks on a little way with Mazur. Jep nudges Dave. "Come on, has she said anything to you?"

Dave swallows hard. "About Mazur? No. Ask *her,* why don't you?"

Mazur goes off and Susan stands alone on the curb. Taking a mirror out of her bag, she examines her face.

Jep chuckles. "Get that. She doesn't know we're watching her. Toot the horn."

Dave taps it lightly.

Susan looks up and sees Dave. She starts running toward him.

Jep pop his head out of the window. "Hey, want a lift?"

Susan stops in confusion, then recovers herself. She comes up to the car with a smile for each of them. "Hey, what'd you guys do, steal a car?"

"Yeah," Jep says, "we're on the lam. Want to take off for Mexico?"

Susan laughs. "Really, whose is it?"

"Mine," Dave says. "I just picked it up."

"The silver VW you told me about the other day! Did you know then you were buying it?"

"Yeah," Dave says. "I wanted to surprise everybody."

Jep elbows him sharply. "You told her and not me?"

"He didn't tell me, he just hinted." Susan comes around to Jep's side. "We bumped into each other downtown Saturday, didn't Dave tell you?"

Jep jabs him again. "No, this guy don't tell me anything! What's going on here?"

"He's got more important things on his mind, I guess."
She opens the door. "I thought you were offering me a
ride."

"We are," Dave says uncertainly. "Want to get in the
back?"

"No, no, in here." Jep pulls her onto his lap and shuts
the door after her. "Okay, blast off!"

Dave starts the car. As they roll down the ramp of the
parking lot, Susan's knee touches his.

"This is great," she says.

She's absolutely right. "There's Willo." Dave honks his
horn.

Willo drops the bag of bats he has slung over his shoulder. "Where'd you get it?" he calls.

"In a raffle." Dave stops the car.

"You're kidding."

"Yeah, I am," Dave says. "I bought it on Saturday."

Willo, ambling over lazily, rests his hands on the
sunroof. "Hey, you got a hole here. Hope they gave you a
discount. Give me a ride sometime?"

"Anytime you say," Dave says. "See you around."

"For sure, man. Good luck!"

Jep hangs out the window. "I hear you're being scouted
by a Yankee farm club, Willo!"

"What?"

Dave smiles as they chug away and leave Willo behind.

"Rides nice," Jep says.

Susan inhales. "And it smells good."

He's done the right thing for once. "Where to?" Dave
asks.

Jep bounces Susan from one knee to another. "Try Sunrise Highway. Let's see this mother go."

10

"Have you tried it on the highway?" Dave's dad is sitting inside the car.

"Yeah, just now. It's good." Dave is still pretty tense. At least they're over the first shock. Dave glances at his mom's face. She doesn't look too thrilled, but she hasn't made a fuss.

Dave's dad listens to the engine again and then turns off the motor.

Dave hesitates for a second. "Want to try it out on the road?"

"Later." His dad gets out of the car. "I don't have my glasses." He shoves his hands in his pockets. "It would have been smart to have a mechanic look it over."

Dave paces. "Yeah, I know. It's just that there wasn't much time."

His mother touches the fender lightly. "What was the rush?"

"The guy was leaving town."

"That's convenient," she says. "And if you need him for anything?"

"What would I need him for?"

"To ask him— Never mind. It's just that old cars are notorious for having things wrong with them. It's insured? You took care of that?"

"Yeah," Dave says, "the guy who sold it to me took me to the insurance office this afternoon."

"When?" his mother asks.

"Don't worry—all I missed was gym and English!"

His mother groans.

"No good, Dave," his dad says, shaking his head.

"It was the only time he could take me. It's my first cut all year!"

"And your last," his dad booms.

"Yeah, yeah, okay."

"We're disappointed," his mom says, "that you didn't come to us about this."

"You'd have stopped me."

She nods. "I guess we'd have tried." She glances at the car again. "I worry about the size of it. There's nothing up there in front, in case—"

"Don't worry, I'll be careful."

"*You* will, but what about the other guy?"

"You and dad have been driving for years and you're still alive!"

His dad prods the fender. "The body isn't too bad."

"I know." Dave smiles appreciatively. "Like the color?"

His dad shrugs. He kneels down. "You're going to need four new tires."

"I know," Dave says quickly. Four tires? Man, how much will that be?

His father gets up. "How much did you pay for it?"

"Seven ninety-five."

His mom winces. "Do you have anything left?"

"A little, plus I'll be starting my job."

"I figure five hundred minimum to make this car safe," his dad says. "Tires, a new clutch. Think you can afford it?"

"Yeah," Dave insists. "I'm going to learn to repair it myself."

His dad looks skeptically at the sunroof. "I'll tell it to you straight. I have very mixed feelings. One part of me says what a mistake! The other part says let him learn a lesson the hard way, that keeping up is harder than getting." His dad looks at his mom. "I learned on that first Ford."

"I remember," she says.

He looks back at Dave. "Did you fill up the gas tank yet?"

"Yeah."

"That's your first lesson in upkeep. One reason I'm taking a calm view of this," he goes on, "is that Fred Staller called me. He can get you the job. He wants to see you tomorrow right after school. Maybe this isn't such a bad idea after all," he says to Dave's mom. "You won't have to be driving him to work all the time."

His mom sighs again. "Just be careful, okay?"

"I will," Dave says. Whew. The worst of it is over.

His dad yawns. "I've got to go inside and pay some bills. Want to keep your new baby in the garage next to Mom's? I don't mind leaving the wagon on the street in nice weather."

"Thanks. Thanks a lot." Dave watches his parents go back into the house. As he stands there, a car stops and his sister gets out.

"So long," she calls. "See you tomorrow!"

Dave hears the sound of her clogs. "Hey, Lisa," he says.

"Dave! Oh, you scared me! What are you doing?"

"Admiring my car."

The *tap-tap* sound stops. "You got one! Incredible!" Then there's a new flurry of *tap*s and Lisa's arms are around his neck. "Where'd you get it? Who from? Do Mom and Daddy know? Give me a ride!"

"Hop in," he says.

Dave drives past the school and then comes back to their street.

Lisa gathers up her things. "Thanks for showing it off. I'm so jealous. I covet it. Teach me to drive?"

"You're fourteen."

"Oh, come on—has Susan seen it yet?"

"Yeah."

She looks at him guardedly. "You like Susan, don't you? Think she likes you?"

He pauses. "There's a chance." Damn it, don't blab to Lisa.

Lisa's expression is earnest as they get out of the car. "What about Jep though? I thought they were going together."

Dave slams the door. "I guess the best man'll win."

Lisa starts up the path. "I hope it's you," she says.

"Thanks." Dave clears his throat. "Don't *say* anything—"

Lisa moans. "Are you kidding? What do you think I am?" She opens the front door. "I have to go in now. Will you drive me to school tomorrow?"

"If you help me sell papers."

"Yeah, sure. Anything for a ride. Good night, lucky duck!"

Dave can't help smiling to himself as she goes into the house. He walks around the car, looking at it one more time. BAT on the license plate—very appropriate. Just what he always wanted, his own Batmobile.

11

The pay phone by the school cafeteria rings. Willo grabs the receiver. "Who? Jacoby? Yeah. Wait a second. Hey, Jacoby—here!"

"For me?" Dave hands his leftover *Carrions* to Susan and makes his way to the phone. "Hello?"

"Hi."

Jepson. Dave strains to hear with all the noise in the background. "Hi. The sale has gone really great. Where are you calling from?"

"Downtown."

"How come? I thought you were going for a ride?"

"I started out."

Dave straightens up. "And? Nothing's wrong, is it?"

Silence.

"Jep? How's the car? Jepson? Where are you?"

"Casey's Body Shop."

Dave's eyes shut. "No, God, no. What happened?"

"It's pretty bad."

"What *happened?* Something with the clutch?"

"*Body* shop, I said."

Dave's voice is weak. "Just tell me, please."

"The Batmobile's totaled. Sorry, man, I'm really—"

Dave stares. He can't move.

"Jacoby?" Jep says. "Jacoby, are you there? Hey, *April Fool*, idiot! I never thought you'd fall for it. The Batmobile's never been better."

Dave lets out his breath. "You swear?"

"By Susan's boobs."

Dave smiles. "You— How could you *do* that? Where are you really?"

"Around the corner. At Gaggy's Pizza. When Susan said no to the beach I didn't feel like going by myself. Want to take a little ride now that sale is over?"

"Now?"

"Yeah. Nicest part of the day."

"I've got *school*, man."

"Go tomorrow."

"I missed English yesterday."

"What are you worrying about? You speak like a native."

"I have an interview at Brite-Lite."

"We'll be back in time."

"No, forget it," Dave says.

"Is Susan there?" Jep asks.

"Yeah."

"Put her on for a second."

Dave motions her over. "Jep wants you," he says.

Susan squeezes close to him and takes the receiver. "Yeah, Jep, what do you want?"

Dave can't help feeling horny. They've never been this close before. He could move away and give her more room, but he doesn't.

"I told you I don't want to cut," Susan says to Jep. "Well, no, only health class. Yeah, but Schultz is giving that quiz. . . ."

Dave, weak kneed, can hear the faint hum of Jep's voice on the other end.

"Yeah, well, okay. Yes, I'm sure he will." Susan closes her palm over the receiver for a moment. "I said we'd go with him," she whispers to Dave, touching her nose to his.

He inhales her minty breath. "Okay. So long as I'm back for Brite-Lite later on."

Susan speaks into the phone. "We'll meet you at Gaggy's in a minute or two, Jep. Yeah, Dave's coming. I talked him into it."

The VW rumbles along Belle Park Avenue. Sunrise Highway is behind them on their way to the beach.

Jep reaches for the radio knob. "It's the Doors—turn it up!"

"There, got it," Dave says. Morrison's voice fills the car.

Jep sings along with Morrison in the front seat next to Dave. Dave wishes he could have figured how to get Susan up front. He can't even see her where she's sitting in the back.

"So the *Carrion* went over big," Jep says as Morrison fades away.

"Yeah." Dave stops for a stop sign. "Too bad you missed out on it. Everybody was reading it in classes all day. They were asking who wrote it. I denied everything."

Susan's face pops up behind them. "Which of you wrote the story about me?"

"Did you like it?" Dave asks.

"Yeah. It was a riot."

"*I wrote it,*" Dave and Jep both say at the same time.

Susan leans forward. "Come on, really, who did?"

"Me."

"Me."

Dave steps on the gas. "We made six bucks after paying for the paper it's printed on."

"Whoopee!" Jep sniffs. "Hey, did any of the big honchos see the masterpiece?"

"Yeah, Richards," Dave says. " 'Dubious taste, but harmless.' That's what he told someone."

Jep smoothes his mustache. "Harmless? We'll have to try harder next year. No problem selling it?"

"No, Susan helped, and my sister and Nan Tobin."

Susan leans forward again. "What's her last name—that girl?"

"Tobin." Dave bears down on the pedal as they hit an open stretch. Houses are sparse now. They pass a service station.

"What do you think of her?" Susan asks.

"Not bad," Jep says. "A little aloof."

"Dave?" Susan's forehead presses the back of his seat.

"She's nice. It's kind of rough for her. She's not used to Belle Park yet."

"How do you know?" Susan asks.

"I was over at her house."

"What are you, the Welcome Wagon?" Puckering her mouth, she imitates Nan.

Dave doesn't notice. "No, no big deal, I just took her the *Carrion* to type."

Susan sits up. "How come you didn't ask me?"

Jep whirls around and grabs her playfully by the wrist. "Because you can't type! Don't sweat it, though. You've got other fine attributes."

Eyes on the road, Dave can't see what Jep is doing now, but whatever it is, he's leaning halfway into the back seat.

Susan is laughing. Dave tries to see in the mirror. "Watch that stuff," he says as casually as he can.

The car bumps over an uneven spot. Jep and Susan slide back into place. "It's going to be so great," Susan says, smoothing her hair back. "This spring and summer—going to the beach. Especially the ocean beach out around Montauk. Can we go sometime soon, Dave?"

"I'll see when I get my work schedule."

Jep elbows him. "You're asking about a job for me? Don't forget to tell them how great I am."

"I know, you're a genius." Dave steadies his foot on the pedal. They're into the long empty stretch now that leads to the town beach.

Susan rests her chin on the back of the seat. "You're making me jealous."

Dave turns to look at her.

"You two, with your jobs. You'll be so filthy rich, and I'll be flat broke."

Jep smiles. "Broke, maybe, but *flat?* Never. Don't worry, we'll share with you."

Dave stares at the road. *We'll share you.* Is that what he just heard?

Suddenly Susan grips Dave's shoulder. "What's that?"

The car wobbles. Jep claps his hands on his knees. "Hey, man, pull over."

Goddamn it. Stopping short with a jolt, Dave gets out on his side and looks at the tire.

Jep jumps out on the other side. "Speaking of *flat.*"

"What is it?" Susan calls.

"Flat, like a panake."

"Can you fix it?" she asks.

"Sure," Jep says.

Dave and Jep eye each other. "Have you ever changed one?" Dave asks.

Jep shakes his head. "Where's the thigamajig?"

"The jack?" Darting around, Dave pulls the hood release. He shouldn't have come here. It was so dumb.

"Hand me the jack," Jep says.

Dave lifts the hood. There's the spare, wedged in tightly, pretty bald-looking. What else? An old shopping bag. No tool kit, no jack. They're stuck here, the way it looks. He'll miss his appointment.

"What's happening?" Susan calls.

Jep gives her a victory sign. "We'll be rolling in no time."

"There's no jack," Dave tells him quietly.

"There must be." Jep searches.

Dave paces nervously. For this he's cutting class again? He may lose the job, too. His parents will kill him. Damn Keith for selling him a car with no jack.

"Only thing to do"—Jep stuffs his hands into his pockets—"is to walk to that Sunoco."

"That was at least a mile back."

Jep shrugs. "We could wait for a lift, but there hasn't been much coming along."

"It figures," Dave says. "Who but *us* goes to the beach on April Fool's Day?"

"Don't bust a gut." Jep pulls out his wallet. "Here. At least my mom left me this this morning. Take it, in case they want cash up front." He hands him ten dollars.

Dave looks at him. "How about *you* going?"

Jep considers. "No, look, if somebody comes by with a jack, I think I can fix it. And if there's a chance of a lift, they'll pick you up quicker."

"How come?"

"You look more all-American, blond, blue-eyed boy!"

Susan's head appears at the window. "What's *happening,* you guys?"

"We're deciding who should stay and protect you!" Jep calls back. "You go, Jacoby, she'll be disappointed if I leave."

Dave feels like challenging that, but what can he say to him? He takes the ten dollars and heads up the road.

12

Dave slides down in his desk chair. His mother's in the kitchen and his sister is in her room, doing aerobic exercises, making a lot of noise. He pulls out the novel from the pile of books from school. No way he can concentrate on reading it tonight. They've discussed it in class for two days now without him, and he hasn't even found time to finish it yet. And that's just one course. Health is another. Who needs to know that somewhere in your guts are the *islets of Langerhans?*

Dave tilts his chair back. He feels like quitting school, the mood he's in. His mom isn't even happy about his working part time. Lucky for him he made it to Brite-Lite while Staller was still there. Otherwise he'd never have heard the end of it from his parents. Dave lets the chair legs come down with a thump. Face it, he's down, too, but it's not his parents' fault. It's this business with Susan. Willo's right, she's just teasing him. Otherwise she'd never have done what she did. When he came back with the service station guy—goddamn, he couldn't believe it. Susan and Jep making out in *his* car. He should have expected it, probably. April Fool's Day—it figures. Still, why does he have to be the biggest fool?

Not worth it, Dave decides, sitting up in the chair

again. Not worth flunking his courses and losing a friend. Forget Susan—the flake. Get back to normal life again. Reaching out for his book, he looks for his place. In another few minutes the phone rings in the hall. He can hear Lisa running and then calling him.

"Dave!"

He doesn't move.

"Dave, telephone!"

He gets up stiffly and drags himself into the hall.

Lisa stands by the phone, one hand on the receiver. Rising on her toes, she wriggles with glee. "It's Susan!" she whispers.

Dave stops long enough to glare with disgust. Then he heads back to his room.

"Dave!" Lisa cries.

"Come off it," he yells. "Tell your retarded friend Pam that I know it's April Fool's Day!"

"Dave—" Lisa comes into his room.

"Get out of here."

But Lisa is determined. Shaking her off, he runs to the phone and hangs up.

"Dave!" Lisa wails.

He considers how to throttle her. Meanwhile the phone rings again. He picks it up. "Quit it, Pam!" he shouts.

"It's Susan, Dave. What's wrong?"

He leans weakly against the wall. "Susan," he says, "I—I'm sorry. Why—? What—?"

"I'm upset. Could we talk?" she asks in a low voice.

"Yeah."

"In person?"

"Where?"

"In your car? In front of my house?"

"When? Right now?"

"Yes," she says. "I'll be watching for you."

Dave pulls up at the curb and turns off his headlights. Someone moves at a window inside the house. Does she know he's here? He waits. Damn it, it's cold. The whole thing is a joke on him, he thinks suddenly, staring into the dark. Then he sees her, it must be her, coming out of the house. Leaning over, he pushes the door open for her.

She gets into the car. "Hi," she says huskily.

"Hi." He can't get a good look at her face. The only light is from a streetlamp two houses down. He's pretty sure she's wearing her new sweater, the pink one. On the other hand, he's not really sure of anything.

Susan turns to him slowly. "You hate me, don't you?"

"Hate you? No, why?"

Susan takes a breath. "I saw the look on your face when you came back this afternoon."

"Hell, I was mad about—" He pauses. "Yeah, I was mad all right. If you've outgrown somebody and you feel like breaking up, then how come you're making out with him in the back of my car?"

Susan sits motionless on the edge of the seat. "I knew it. That's why I called you up. I couldn't take having you not understand."

"Not understand *what?*"

She drops her hands to her lap. "Understand that I love you and not Jep."

Dave sits very still.

Susan stares straight ahead. "You probably wish I'd just go take a walk."

"No," he says softly, "that's not what I wish."

Susan strokes her sweater with her hand. "I've been giving you hints. Today made me see that I have to speak up. I should tell Jep, I know," she says, on the edge of tears. "I'd have told him already if it was anyone but you I loved."

Dave still doesn't move. Loved, she said. Love.

Susan shivers. "When you left for the gas station this afternoon, I thought *good,* this is the perfect time. I'll *tell* him. If you'd been there you'd seen why I couldn't. First he said how bad I've been treating him, and then he said this really sad thing."

"What?"

"He said he doesn't have a family." Susan stops for a second. "But it doesn't really bother him because he's got us. Me and you—you're like a brother, he said."

"He wasn't hamming it up?"

"No, it was sad!" Susan sways back and forth. "The way he came out with it, I couldn't say good-bye to him. That's when he put his arms around me, and you came back at that point." She turns her face. "Hate me if you want to, but I couldn't hurt his feelings."

"I don't hate you," Dave says. "I've loved you since seventh grade."

Susan looks up. "Really?" She smiles. "That long? Oh, God, Dave, what should we do?"

Dave can see her eyes now, and he feels her hand touching his. "If it were me in his place, I'd want to be told."

Susan squeezes his hand. "But you aren't him, you aren't! He's much crazier than you. You could take it; he can't."

"Meaning what? You'll keep going with him and I'll tag along with you?"

"I'll end it," Susan says, sinking back in the seat. "I'll think of a way."

Dave hunches. "Meanwhile?"

"Meanwhile"—Susan leans close to him—"you're starting that job."

"Tomorrow," he says as she snuggles closer to him.

"How often will you work? What time will you go there?"

"Three days a week at three o'clock and all day on Saturday as long as school's on. Why?"

"I'll meet you when you get out of work as often as I can, okay?"

Dave fiddles with the wheel. "We'll be making a jerk of him."

"No, we won't," Susan says. "It'll just be *at first*. I'll be ending it gradually. If the three of us go out, I'll bring another girl along, so it'll look like a foursome. He'll think the other girl's for you."

"Thanks a lot," Dave says grimly.

"What else can we do?"

"*I* could tell him."

"That would be real brotherly."

"It would be, more than this is."

Susan shakes her head. "Wait a while, please."

Dave leans back wearily. "I'm not waiting long. Staller said when school's over he can give Jep a job. You can't meet me at work when Jep's right *there*."

Susan hugs him. "I promise, it'll be over way before then."

Dave pulls her closer, into a circle of light. He looks at her with awe. "I don't believe this."

She grins at him. "What?"

"Any of it," he says.

"Was it really since seventh grade? Why didn't you tell me?"

"Too shy." He presses his lips to hers.

"No more, though." She smiles.

"I guess not." He kisses her hard.

13

Dave picks up a flashlight and wipes it with a cloth. Then another and another as the belt brings them on. While he cleans them, he glances at the clock on the wall. Five-twenty. Ten more minutes and he's through for the day.

The hum suddenly stops and the belt rattles to a halt. While he can, Dave sneaks a look at the Brite-Lite parking lot. There's the Batmobile all alone—Susan hasn't come yet. She will, though. The belt hums again and Dave grabs a plastic tube. What day is it? Wednesday. Damned hot for June, he thinks. What'll it be like in the dead of summer? He and Jep will begin to find out when they start this coming Monday, full-time.

They need the bucks, that's for sure. Gas alone is costing a fortune. Plus paying off the loan from his parents for the clutch and the tires. At least his mom is off his back now that the car is safe to drive. How did he get along before he had the Batmobile? Without it, he and Susan would be—well, they'd be nowhere.

Staring at the conveyor belt, Dave tries to concentrate. He can't manage it, though. He keeps thinking of her and what they'll do when she comes. Usually they don't talk much—they just rush into his car and start fooling around. Once they almost *did it,* but he's glad he held back. First of all, he'd feel guilty as hell about Jep. Second, he'd prefer feeling a little surer of himself. The main reason they don't talk much is they don't want to discuss Jep. After nearly two months like this, Jep still doesn't know what's going on. Dave has decided this is it, though. They can't keep stringing him along. Jep's planning something special tonight for his anniversary with Susan, for God's sake.

Here comes Staller, checking his work. Staller picks up a tube. "This one is still greasy."

"I'm sorry." Dave wipes it again.

Staller smiles. "Watch 'em closer, okay?" He pauses. "What do you say, Dave, do you like working here?"

"Yeah, I do. I'm really sorry—"

"Forget it this time." He looks at Dave sympathetically. "Worrying about your exams? Go on—leave early today."

"Thanks, Mr. Staller!"

Dave is out in the parking lot with the sun beating down on him. Susan must have just gotten here—she's sitting in his car. He sneaks up, opens the door, and hugs her before she can turn around. She presses close to him for a second and then pulls back.

"Guess what. Jep's taking us to Nassau Coliseum tonight." She rolls her eyes upward. "For our *first anniversary*—isn't that a laugh? He's got four tickets to Southside Johnny, and he wants you to come."

Dave lets go of her. "No."

"What do you mean *no*?"

He fingers the steering wheel. "What I said. Go ahead and celebrate. I'm staying home."

"He has four tickets!"

"Good. Invite Willo and Mazur."

"Dave, *why?*"

He shakes his head. "I can't do it."

"Can't do what? How can we say no? He went to the trouble—he's paying for you and Nan!"

"Nan? Nan Tobin?"

"Yes," Susan says. "Wasn't that a brainstorm? She's the first person I ran into, and I asked her to come. It'll look so right to Jep. He knows Nan is a friend of yours."

Dave slumps. "Did you have to pick Nan?"

"I didn't *pick* her," Susan says impatiently. "I told you, she's the first person I saw. What's wrong with it? She's excited about going!"

Dave lets out his breath. "That's exactly the point. She thinks she's my date, right?"

"Well, yes, but so what? I explained it's the four of us."

"It's a crummy thing to do!"

"Why?" Susan narrows her eyes. "Is there something I don't know here? Does she have a *thing* for you? Are you attracted to her?"

Dave fingers the steering wheel. "She's a nice girl is all. And I don't like the idea of using her."

"How is she being used? She's seeing Southside Johnny for free! What's wrong with that?"

Dave shuts his eyes. "It's all settled? She said yes, definitely?"

"Yes."

He opens his eyes again. "The only reason I'm going to go tonight is so she won't feel like an idiot."

"Not for me you're not going?" Susan presses her forehead to his chest. "Please don't be mad, Dave. I'm sorry I asked her. I had no idea you'd feel this way. I should have asked Mindy—"

"No, no, leave it like it is," Dave says. "But never again, I swear—"

Susan hugs him. "Of course *never again*. I'm telling Jep as soon as we get past this. I'll tell him Friday. By then school will be over and maybe he'll be mellowed out."

"Friday at the latest?"

Susan nods her head against his chest. "Tonight won't be bad," she says, nuzzling him with her chin. "We'll be pretending for the last time." She tilts her face upward. "Just don't put on *too* good an act with Nan, or I'll die of jealousy. Look at me once in a while tonight, okay?" Leaning forward, she kisses him.

"Not more than once a minute," Dave says as their lips part and then meet again.

"Hey, Southside, don't go 'way yet!"

Dave deflects a flying paper cup before it hits Nan. "Bunch of rowdies," he says. "This is going to be some intermission." He and Nan, standing close to the stage, are caught in the moving crowd. Susan and Jep—where the hell did they get to? . . . Right beside them a minute ago. Good, there's Susan. He starts to smile, but her dark look makes him quit. "Where's Jep?" He mouths the words across the heads of the spectators between them.

Shrugging with annoyance, Susan mumbles, "He *went* somewhere. Let's get out of this."

Dave beckons her, and with one hand on Nan's shoulder, he steers them through the crowd. "What do you think of the concert?" he asks Nan. "Pretty much what you expected?"

"It's wild," Nan shouts in his ear. "The music is okay, but it's the energy that's so amazing!"

Elbows jab Dave in the ribs as he tries to make head-way.

"Wait!" Susan calls, and he grabs her by the hand. Jerking her way forward, she squeezes his fingers hard.

He looks at her. "What?"

"Do you have to keep *touching* Nan?"

He stares at her, puzzled. "What the—? I don't want to lose her!"

"That's obvious," Susan says, letting go of his hand.

Meanwhile Nan has slipped free and is motioning them toward her. The three of them huddle near a red exit sign. "What happened to Jep?" Nan asks Susan.

"Take one guess."

"Men's room?" Dave says.

"No, guess again." She folds her arms. "He saw Bull Curtis somewhere around here. Bull's selling bottles."

"Bottles?"

"Vodka. Just what Jep needs, right?" Susan's voice is heavy with sarcasm. "He's got so much to celebrate." She gives Dave a sideways glance. "Maybe you and I should go and find him."

"In this madhouse?" Dave pauses, realizing he's missed the cue to get away with her. "I don't think—"

"What's the problem?" Susan asks coolly. "I'm sure Nan wouldn't mind waiting here."

Dave sees that Nan, embarrassed, is glancing away, pretending not to hear. "Jep'll be back," he says. "No point bucking the crowd."

Susan glares. "Do what you want, then. I'll go myself."

"Wait." Dave tries to stop her, but when she keeps going, he watches her go.

"What's happening?" Nan asks.

"They're having troubles," Dave says. "I'm sort of—in the middle. I'm sorry about this, I mean for your sake."

Nan shrugs. "Don't worry about that part. I'm not sorry I came. I knew this wouldn't be *usual.*" She smiles. "Since when does Susan Scherra invite *me* along?"

"It's complicated." Dave meets her eyes. "I'm glad you came, actually. It's good *somebody's* enjoying Southside, after Jep spent those bucks. He must have borrowed from his mother. He's been planning this anniversary."

"It's interesting that he bought four tickets," Nan says. "As if he didn't want Susan and him to be all alone."

"Yeah, I didn't think of it that way before."

Nan pauses. "You two must be close."

Dave looks at her quickly.

"You and Jep, I mean."

"Yeah, yeah we are."

"Here comes Susan." Nan gives a nod.

Susan appears, rolling her eyes. "I found him, *unfortunately.* He's on his way back with his bottle. I swear I feel like leaving." She whispers to Dave, "Is there any way you could take me home?"

"No, we're sticking it out." He guides Nan with his hand again. "Intermission's over. Let's move back where we were."

Caught in the swell, they're pushed to the spot near the stage where Jep waits with a brown bag clutched in one hand. In the few minutes before the music resumes, Dave can see him arguing with Susan and taking long swigs from the bottle that is inside the bag. Hell, forget them both, he thinks to himself. Nan is enjoying this. Don't spoil it for her.

"Hey, Southside!" the crowd yells.

The fans clap and thump their fists. Johnny takes the

stage again, bathed in purple light. Now the Jukes join in, their shadows writhing behind them. The spots turn orange, then yellow, then white. The whole audience sways. Dave feels more relaxed than he's been in a long time. He looks at Nan and laughs as the crush of the crowd brings them closer.

The last set now and the longest—"I Don't Want to Go Home!" the fans sing. Johnny strips off his tight black jacket and throws it into the crowd. Finally the music winds down and the audience breaks up. Dave, steering Nan as before, makes sure that Susan and Jep are behind them. The four of them push through the doors and come out on the parking lot, where headlights blind their eyes and car horns blare in their ears.

"Wait," Dave says to Nan, while Susan and Jep catch up with them.

"I loved it," Nan tells Jep. "Thanks for inviting me—it was great."

"Yeah, man," Dave nods. "I appreciated it."

Jep looks blearily from Nan to Dave as they make their way down through the rows of cars. "Thanks. Nice when friends *appreciate*. Not everybody does." Glaring at Susan, he lifts the bag to his lips again. "Some anniversary."

Susan's face is like stone.

Jep nudges her. "Who is it? Come on, may as well tell me."

"You're drunk." Susan veers away. "Here's the car. Let's go home."

"Let's go home." Jep mocks her voice. Leaning against the Batmobile, he downs the rest of the vodka and holds the bottle over his head. "Happy anniversary!" he yells, throwing the bottle in the air.

Susan and Nan stare, disbelieving. Dave tries to follow

the thing with his eyes. It lands with a splat and a tinkle between two parked cars.

"Idiot!" Susan sniffs.

Dave unlocks the car and opens the other door from the inside. Susan rushes around and gets into the front seat.

Jep, still holding onto the car, tries to ease the keys from Dave's hands. "I'll drive, okay?"

"No, I will," Dave says.

"I'm not drunk," Jep insists. "Come on, I got to talk to her."

"You'd better drive," Nan tells Dave.

"Yeah, come on, man," Dave says.

Jep looks at Dave pleadingly. "I'm fine. Give me a break. I trust *you,* don't you trust *me?*"

Reluctantly Dave pushes the driver's seat forward and follows Nan into the back.

Jep gets behind the wheel and starts up the car with a jolt. The Batmobile moves forward, narrowly missing another car.

"Watch it!" Susan says.

"I'm watching," Jep mutters as horns beep.

"You're acting crazy!"

"I ought to be!" He cuts off another car. "Who *was* it? Not going to tell me?" Jep turns to the back seat. "Know what I heard tonight? *This* one's been fooling around," he says. "Curtis *saw* her. How do you like that?"

"You're drunk," Susan says.

Dave shuts his eyes and sinks down.

Jep, facing forward, cuts into the front of a long line of cars. "I'll show you how sober I am. Kiddies, watch this."

Dave feels Nan's arm braced rigidly against his. An attendant blows a whistle, but Jep doesn't stop.

He sails out of the lot now, onto the soft shoulder of the road.

Nan says evenly, "Come on, Jep. Let Dave drive. It's his car."

"But he *shares*. He's a buddy. This guy's my best friend!"

Dave slips farther down in the seat.

"What are you trying to prove?" Susan shouts at Jep.

"I just want to get home! Lay off, okay?"

As the Batmobile rattles along, passing cars on the right, Dave stares straight ahead. What else did Bull say? He expects Jep to start questioning again, but to his surprise Jep keeps quiet. Dave avoids looking at Susan and Nan. He can feel his heart pounding.

At some point Jep gets back onto the road, and Dave can hear Nan breathe easier. What's Jep going to do now? They're back in Belle Park. He takes the curve fast on Harrison and then zooms onto Franklin. He stops in front of his house and gets out of the car.

"Tomorrow," he says to Susan, "we'll discuss this, you and me." When he's out on the curb he turns to Susan one more time. "If I find out who it is, I'll kill the guy, I swear I will." He calls in through the window to Dave, "Sorry about this whole scene, man. Take her home for me, please. I'm too mad to look at her."

In a trance Dave climbs in the front and drives straight to Susan's house. When he gets there, he tells Nan, "Excuse me a minute." Letting Susan out, he walks her up the path as far as the front steps.

"Where do you think Bull saw us?" Susan whispers with a smile.

"I don't know and I don't care." Dave takes a step

backward. "Susan, listen—count me out from now on."

Her mouth twitches. "What do you mean?"

"Tell him or don't tell, whatever you want to do. But I'm not seeing you anymore. I decided tonight."

Susan tries to touch his hand, but Dave backs away farther. "I mean it," he says. "It's gotten to be too much. 'Bye." And he hurries back to the car.

As he drives away, he's shaking a little. Nan notices, he's pretty sure. "You must wonder what the hell's going on."

Nan's slow to answer. "I figure you'll tell me if you want to. I could guess, but I won't. One thing—you've had it with her, am I right?"

"Yeah. I've been a jerk for a long time, but I'm finished." Dave feels wiped out, too tired to talk. He drives on to her street and then walks her to her house. "I hope you didn't have too bad a time. Maybe some other night, when I'm more up for it—"

"I'd like that," Nan says. "See you tomorrow at the exam."

14

Dave stirs as he listens to the tick of the clock. Another half hour and they've got to hand their papers in. He's finished with the vocabulary and the fill-in-the-blanks, but the essays on the novels—he just can't concentrate. It wouldn't be so hard if Susan wasn't here. There she is, looking over at him every once in a while. Lucky that Jep's taking math, so he's in another room.

Dave can't think of anything else. No two ways about it—he's going to tell Jep after the exam: *I didn't mean to go behind your back, but it's over, I swear.*

Susan's looking at him again. Dave focuses on the test. He's glad he's through with her, he realizes. There's more that's real between him and Jep than between him and her. He *likes* Jep more. How did he get into this mess?

Unexpectedly, Susan gets up and hands in her exam. She's finished. She's leaving. Dave watches her go. New jeans she's wearing—tight, like in the TV ads. Hooking her bag over her shoulder, she gives him another look. Turning away to avoid her eyes, Dave returns to the test. Meanwhile the door opens and closes and Susan is gone.

"All papers in now. Have a good summer."

Dave, scribbling his last sentence, takes his time getting up. Susan may be waiting for him, but he's determined to give her the slip. The main thing is to find Jep and get everything off his chest. Nan Tobin, he notices, is looking his way now. "Hi," he says to her as he hands in his paper.

"Hi. How do you think you did?"

"Lousy. Too much junk on my mind. What about you?"

"Oh, I think I probably did okay," Nan says. "So you're still feeling bad."

"Yeah. I want to see Jep alone. You'll excuse me if I—?"

"Go. I hope everything works out."

Dave squeezes Nan's elbow as he turns to go away. "Thanks. I'll tell you what this is all about sometime soon. Can I give you a call?"

"Sure."

"Okay, so long." Dave goes into the hall. No Susan, thank God. If he sees her, he'll run.

A hand grabs him from behind. "Jacoby, how's it going?"

"Willo!"

"Yeah, who'd you think it was? Hey, poker game at my house tonight. Can you come?"

"Tonight?"

"Got something better to do?"

Dave hesitates. "No."

"About eight. Mazur's coming and Tom Pritchard. We can count you in, right? Bring your piggy bank along."

Dave considers. "Yeah, okay."

"Great," Willo says. "Where're you headed now?"

"I'm looking for Jepson. It's kind of important—"

"Catch you later."

Dave crosses the street. Let him meet up with Jep quick. He goes by the section where the Mopeds are parked, but he doesn't see Jep's, so he walks toward his car. As soon as he sees the Batmobile, he realizes something is wrong. The way it's sagging—what the hell? Oh, no, *not again.* His new left front tire is flat, and it looks as if—goddamn! The right rear is flat, too. No way this was an accident. He stands for a minute in the early afternoon sun. At the far end of the lot a few kids are hanging out. It couldn't be them or they'd have beat it. He considers going over and asking what they know. He should report this in school, but he can't deal with that.

So he walks in a daze toward the nearest service station. Jep found out, Dave decides, and this is what he did. It isn't Jep's style exactly, but he probably went wild. Dave isn't mad. He feels sick. It means they're finished as friends.

"What time is it?" Dave asks the service-station attendant.

"Three-fifteen. You're all set."

"Thanks." Dave looks at his tires. Inflated again. "How much do I owe you?"

"Five dollars for my time. Sorry you had to wait, but I couldn't leave the station any sooner."

Dave pays him.

The attendant gets into his truck. "I'd report that," he says, starting up and driving off.

Dave sits in the Batmobile. The school parking lot is deserted. What a way to start vacation—he almost wishes he had to go to work. What a rotten thing for Jep to do, though he doesn't really blame him. Even now he'd like to see him and try talking things out. He drives home distractedly, and when he gets there he goes upstairs. Nobody's home, so he heads for his room and stretches out on the bed. She wasn't worth it, is all he can think of. The trip with Jep will be off now. Dave closes his eyes—he'd love to sleep and forget this whole mess.

He sits up abruptly. The phone is ringing in the hall. It's his mother, most likely. He rolls off the bed and picks up the phone. "Yeah," he says, annoyed.

"Where the hell have you been, man? I started calling two hours ago."

"Jep."

"*Yeah*. What are you doing?"

Dave pauses. "What about you?"

"I just got out of school. Coming out of the exam, Richards catches me with a butt! He made me stay in his office. I called you from there. What are you doing?"

"I was sleeping. Before that I had—car trouble."

"What happened?"

"You don't know?"

"How could I? Is it bad?"

"Two flat tires."

"Two?"

"Somebody let the air out."

"Lousy. It happened to another kid yesterday. You didn't report it to Richards?"

"Not yet."

"Do it, man. Lousy break. No damage, though?"

"No, just deflated. I got the guy from the Gulf station to come over and pump them up." Dave wipes his sweaty hand on the front of his shirt. "Uh—you haven't—how *are* you today?"

"After last night? Not bad. I'm going on the wagon. I promised Susan."

"You spoke to her?"

"Yeah, this morning before the exam. I apologized like mad. Curtis was putting me on about her seeing somebody, I'm convinced. He's not called 'Bull' for nothing, right?"

Dave clears his throat. "Look, we've got to talk."

"We're *talking.*"

"In person."

"Why, you know something?"

Dave leans against the wall. "Put it this way: Maybe I do, but don't worry—*it's over.*"

"What's over?"

"When I see you I'll tell you."

"Tonight then, okay? I'm trying to get up a beach party."

"Who with?"

"Susan and Mindy, you—"

"I can't."

"How come?"

"I'm playing poker with Willo."

"Change your plans."

"No. What are you doing right now?"

"Going over to Susan's," Jep says. "She asked me to come over. Why?"

"Nothing. Forget it. I'll see you as soon as you're free. Call me, okay? I'll be home until eight tonight and tomorrow until three."

"You won't change your mind about the beach?"

"No. If I don't hear from you later this afternoon, see you tomorrow before I go to work. My last day by myself, man. From Monday on we'll be in it together."

"I'm looking forward to it."

"So am I," Dave says. "Thanks for calling. So long."

Willo, glancing at his cards, slides two chips toward the pot. "I'm raising, you guys. What's that sound, rain?"

"Yeah, cats and dogs." Mazur tilts back his chair. "I can't believe it—we're seniors."

"It's *summer.*" Pritchard yawns. "We're not nothing until fall. Go on, Mazur, what do you say?"

Mazur scans his cards. "I'll stay." He shoves in his chips.

"Me too," Pritchard says. "You're on, Jacoby."

Dave takes a swig of his Coke. "Raise."

"Is he bluffing?"

"Not Jacoby! Okay, *show,* man. What've you got?"

Dave spreads his cards on the table.

"Full house!" Willo shouts. "Jacoby's too much. How much are you up?"

Dave pulls the pot toward him. "About twenty-five bucks."

"I'm winning it back from you." Mazur shuffles the deck.

Pritchard opens a soda. "Let's play spit-in-the-ocean next."

"I got to go soon," Dave says.

"Come on, not yet." Mazur deals the cards.

Willo arranges his hand. "Jacoby isn't like you guys. He quits while he's ahead."

"I should," Dave says. "But what the hell—one more game. School's over."

"Ain't he the wild one?" Pritchard rolls his eyes. Rain splatters the windows as they push in their chips. Willo, slouching, smiles contentedly. "Zowee," he says.

"Faker."

"Faker, my ass." Willo sits up as the doorbell rings. "Who the hell's that?" He puts down his cards. "Wait a second—I don't trust you guys. I'm taking these with me." Picking up his cards, he goes to the door.

"Are you working this summer?" Dave starts to ask Pritchard.

"Jacoby!" Willo calls.

"Yeah?"

"Come here."

"Why, what's happening?" Dave pushes his chair back. Before he can get up, Jep barges into the room.

Mazur grins. "Look what Willo drug in. Pull up a chair, Jepson, join the next hand."

Jep, head and shirt drenched, keeps coming at Dave. His eyebrows are knitted together. He puts up his fists.

Willo tries to block him off, but Jep lunges at Dave. "Come on outside, Jacoby," he says in a hoarse voice.

"It's pouring rain!" Willo tells him.

"The guy's looped again," Mazur says.

Dave, on his feet now, holds Jepson off. "Hey, what's wrong, how about it?"

"You know goddamn well," Jep says, pummeling Dave's chest with his fists.

Willo and Pritchard pull him away, and soon he stops as if he's worn out. Mazur sniffs. "Give him coffee."

"No, I'll take him home," Dave says.

"You'll bust up the game!" Pritchard complains.

"So what?" Willo says. "Jepson needs to get home. Want help?" he asks.

"No, thanks. I'm experienced." Dave takes half of Jep's weight on his shoulder. "Sorry, you guys. Some other time, okay?" They lurch out the door.

"Sure you don't need any help?" Willo calls.

"I'm sure." Dave closes the door behind them. Rain is coming down steadily so that Dave can barely see his car. He keeps supporting Jep as they sway across the porch. "You smell like a brewery, man."

Suddenly Jep yanks Dave's arm and pulls him down the steps. "I've been drinking because I've been *had.*"

Dave feels cold rain soaking his shirt.

Jep thrusts his chin close to Dave's. "She told me. *You've* been messing with her!"

Locked in Jep's hold, spiraling down the walk, Dave doesn't resist him. "It's over. It was crummy of me. I've been trying to explain!"

"Explain what? How you *did it* with her?"

"We didn't! We *didn't.*"

They're at the edge of the lawn now. Jep weaves toward the curb. "How do *I* know that? Anyway, I don't want to *talk.*" He raises both fists again. "Only one way to go, man. Come on, put 'em up."

Dave squints through the rain. Jep's all show, like a little kid. "Wait a minute," he says.

Winding up, Jep misses Dave. He charges again. Dave sidesteps and Jep goes tumbling to the soggy ground. Jep picks himself up and comes charging one more time. Dave, standing still, feels Jep's head ram his chest hard.

"Gotcha!" Jep gloats.

Dave gasps and waits for more.

But Jep staggers backward. "That'll teach you," he says.

As Dave watches, Jep's knees buckle. Dave catches him in midair. For a second they're locked together and Dave could swear Jep's hugging him.

Dave returns the hug. "I'm sorry," he says. "God, I'm so sorry."

" 'S okay." Jep's full weight is on him.

"We'll talk, okay? Tomorrow."

Jep, nodding, starts slipping again. Then Dave drags

him over the lawn and the sidewalk to the car. With rain in his eyes, in the dark, Dave shoves Jep into the front seat.

His shoes squish as he walks around, climbs in, and digs for his keys. He turns on the engine and flips on the inside lights. "Hey, man, you awake?" he asks, but Jep doesn't answer. It's only then, while Dave is shaking some of the rain out of his hair, that he looks in the rearview mirror and sees Susan's face.

15

Dave shuts off the motor and turns around.

"Hi," Susan says. "I'm so relieved you're all right."

The wave that comes over him is half anger, half excitement. "What are you doing here?"

"I was with Jep and he made me come with him."

Dave stares at her.

"What was he doing to you?" she asks. "I tried to stop him from going into Willo's, but I couldn't. He told me, 'Get in Dave's car and wait for me there!'"

Dave keeps on studying her. Damp hair clings to her cheeks.

She brushes her hair back. "I told him about us. We were down at the beach by ourselves—nobody else could come. He was about to give me this anniversary present and I finally got up the nerve."

Dave looks away.

"Don't you want to hear what happened? I did this for *you*, you know. He didn't believe me at first—"

"I told you, I'm finished!"

"I know you said that last night, but please take it back! When I told him again, he pulled out this bottle of—"

Dave, watching her intently, catches something in her voice. Was it always there? he wonders. She's *enjoying* this mess. "Let's get out of here," he says.

"Wait, listen to the rest. He made me get on the Moped. Then he drove like a maniac. By then, it was starting to rain. I asked him 'Where are we going?' 'I'm going to kill the guy,' he told me. I was *frantic.*"

Dave looks down at Jep sleeping. "Well, he didn't, as you can see."

"I thought he meant it!" Susan looks at herself in the rearview mirror again.

Damn, all she can think of is how she looks. "Where's the Moped?" Dave asks her.

"In Willo's garage, Jep wanted it out of the rain. Was he outrageous in Willo's house?"

Dave starts the car. "No more than usual."

"Where are we going?" Susan asks.

Dave seethes as he pulls out. "Home."

"Take him home first," she says.

Is he tempted? Dave steps on the gas. "No, thanks. I'm taking you first."

Susan rises in her seat. "I don't believe this. I left Jep for you!"

"I'm finished!" The windshield is streaked with rain. Beside him Jep's head bobbles to one side. Dave tries to hoist him up. Which way will be quickest? Harrison onto Belle Park Avenue. It's stuffy in here now. He rolls down his window so that wind and rain blow in his face. What's she doing in the back? *Fixing her makeup.* Dave swerves around a car that is waiting to make a turn.

"Watch it," Susan warns.

"I *am,*" he says testily.

Susan makes a little sound. "You *used* to be nice."

"*Used* to," he agrees, splashing through a puddle.

"*Watch* it," Susan fumes. "I already had one close call tonight."

"And you loved it," Dave says.

"You're horrible."

Dave tries to stay cool. "You don't like *me,* you never did. What you like is these scenes."

"You're awful! You don't appreciate at all what I did!"

"What you did was for youself. All you want is kicks."

Susan's voice drops in pitch. "If that was true I'd stick with Jep. He's much more exciting than you are—don't kid yourself."

Dave tips the rearview mirror, trying to see her expression.

"What are you doing?" she asks.

He isn't really sure.

"Watch the road," Susan says.

Instead he's watching her reflection. As his eyes shift from the mirror to the road, he feels her hand on his back.

"Look out, Dave!" she screams.

Dave slams his feet on the clutch and brake, but it isn't any use. The Batmobile goes wild—it skids, then it flies. Susan's scream becomes shrill. That's the last thing he knows.

Until . . . how long? Where is he? Pant leg wet. It's so dark now. Sobbing—who is it? Dave gropes with both hands. Steering wheel all busted. What happened? Susan! Jep? Dave reaches, feels a hairy leg. Hey, man, that you? He fumbles, then gropes again. Come on, let's get out of here. Too hard to fight it, though. He'll take a snooze, like Jep.

But the whimpering gets more pitiful. Dave, reaching again, this time feels Susan's foot.

"Help," she sobs.

"Yeah." Can't see for anything. What's that? Something jagged. Beyond that a fine mist. "One second," he says, breathless. He hoists himself up.

"Help," Susan whimpers again.

He finds the door, but it won't open. He shoves against it with his shoulder. Still nothing. He grabs the handle and cranks. Glass tinkles and flakes all over him.

"Help me," Susan begs.

His head is jammed somehow. "Where are you?" he asks. "Wait." He can move his leg—now both legs are free. He wriggles his chest and pushes with his hands so his hips go through a slot. Sharp things snag his shirt and his shoulders resist, but he lands on both feet. Hey, he's standing up. Reaching back inside, he feels Susan's hands gripping his. "It's okay," he tells her, and suddenly he's got strength.

As he lifts her, he scraps his arm on glass. Oh, God—it's ripped open. He has to let her down quickly, biting his cheek so he won't yell.

"Don't let me go," she pleads.

Dave sits her on the ground. "Stay here," he says shakily. Okay, Jepson, you're next. Is that you, man? Quit making that noise!

Where's the other window? Dave searches, but all he feels is something solid. Roll it down, man, or I'll have to smash it! He slips in the thick mud. Dave pounds on something twisted. Say something, boozehound! He'll have to try from the other side. Dave staggers to his feet. Dim light from the road glints on the Batmobile. Dave stands and stares at it. It's flipped over on its side, Jep's side sunk in the mud.

Get him out! Not so easy. Dave slips again as he crawls around. Susan is still sobbing. Goddamn it, arm stings like hell. Dave makes it back to the window where he and Susan got out before. "Jepson?" No answer. Instead this roaring sound. Red lights. What's going on here? Doors slam. A siren wails.

It's a blur now. Dave tries to speak.

"Anybody hear me?" someone calls.

"Yeah," Dave answers. A light blinds him. Now they're lifting him head first. He struggles. "Get Jepson," he mumbles.

Someone restrains him. "Don't move."

Dave blinks. It's a cop. "Get my buddy—he's in there."

"Take it easy." The cop holds him. "You were driving?"

"Yeah."

"What happened? Remember anything?"

"I was—Susan?" he shouts.

"She's okay. Your girl friend's fine. How's that leg, hurt bad?" The cop slits the pant leg. "Don't see anything. Hey, lie still."

Dave wrenches. "Get Jepson!" They've got him strapped now, he can't move.

"There were three of you?" The cop stands up. "Hey, Polifrone!"

Meanwhile Dave feels himself being raised off the ground.

"Polifrone, come here!"

Polifrone comes over and shines a light inside the car. While Dave watches, Polifrone shuts his eyes. "My God," he says.

16

Fluorescent lights blazing. Who the hell's here? His mom and dad. There's an eerie sound like in a dream: *Dr. Kraft, Dr. Kraft.* Now somebody's touching him. Where are his pants?

"Is that *his* blood on his jeans?"

"No, the other boy's," someone says.

Dave twitches. "Where's Jep?"

"In the O.R."

What's the O.R.?

"Lie still, please."

"Help the nurse, Dave." His mom's voice.

"Where's Susan?" he asks.

"Susan's fine. Her parents took her home."

His father leans close. "They're asking what you had to drink—"

"Nothing," Dave mumbles. "A Coke or two!"

"They want to know if you're willing to take the blood-alcohol test."

"Maybe he shouldn't," his mom says.

Dave tries to sit up. "Let me—I wasn't drinking."

The doctor holds him down. "Easy now. Relax."

"I wasn't drunk!" Dave repeats.

"Let him take the test," his dad says.

What test are they talking about, the English exam? Did he flunk?

His mom holds his hand. "If you think it'll help him, let them give him the blood test."

Dave feels a cold swab touch his arm. "Let me see Jep."

"Tomorrow."

Dave twitches again but the doctor holds him firmly. He feels the jab of a needle. After that he fades out.

He's somewhere else now. They've moved him, but where to? He hears voices whispering. "Mom? That you, Dad?" Wait a minute—don't call them. It isn't them, anyway. Through a doorway he can see a rectangle of gray light. Groping with one hand, he feels a sheet and a thin gown. His ass is bare. Right arm padded with some kind of cloth. It hurts. Oh, God, no. The Batmobile—still on its side? He can't stay here, for God's sake. He's got to get Jepson out!

Dave struggles with the straps that are keeping him down in bed. Someone's coming. He lies back and pretends he's asleep. Eyes closed, he feels a hand touch him lightly on the wrist.

"Do you want anything, Dave?"

He opens his eyes. Susan? No, not Susan. Some other girl he's never seen before. "Can you untie this?" he asks.

"In the morning. Would you like a sleeping pill?"

Yeah, yeah he would. When she holds the cup to his lips, he takes the pill and gulps it down. "Susan?" he says, confused, but already she's gone. He's almost asleep when the voices begin again. This time they're talking about him. *He shouldn't have . . . His best friend!* Now they're yelling *Watch out!* and he's flying like a crazy man. He's slipping in mud. . . . This is his last chance to save Jep.

He grabs the rear bumper of the car and rocks it until it's upright again. Then he opens the door. Jep lies there, limp. Oh, God, no. Dave bites his lip. Then Jep jumps up, smiling. "Hey, what's the matter? Fooled you, didn't I, man?"

Sunlight dapples the sheet when Dave opens his eyes this time. His eyelids are heavy. The sun is too bright.

A nurse unfastens the strap. "Do you know where you are?" she asks.

"I think so," Dave says. He tries to sit up.

"Let me help." The nurse cranks up the bed for him. "Your parents are here."

"Hi," his dad says. His mother leans over and kisses him. He can't see very well with the sun in his eyes like this. His parents come closer and someone else joins them.

"Dave, Dr. Kraft."

"Hello, Dave."

"Hello."

"How're you feeling?"

That's the *doctor*—that young guy? "Okay," Dave says.

"We're going to release you this morning. But first—"

"Dave—" his dad says.

His mother interrupts too. "Dr. Kraft says your arm will be fine. A superficial scratch is all it is. You passed the blood-alcohol test." Her voice starts to shake. "Susan went home last night—"

"What about Jepson?"

His parents sway over the bed. Dr. Kraft coughs. "Dave, your friend didn't make it."

Make what? Dave looks up. *"Jep,* I'm talking about."

As Dr. Kraft nods slowly, Dave's mother holds her throat. Dave stares from one to the other and then looks Kraft in the eye.

"There was internal bleeding," Kraft says. "We did all

we could. He died early this morning. His mother was with him."

Dave's mom stifles a sob. "We know how you must feel!"

"But it wasn't your fault." His dad sounds like he's about to choke. "It could have happened to anyone—slick road, a bad spot. I've already called Larry Krim, Dave. He'll represent us. They have to ask you some questions down at the station later on."

Dave watches motes of light dance on his bed. A cartful of trays rattles out in the hall. They're still standing by his pillow. His mom's eyes are glazed with tears. His dad keeps on talking, but Dave tunes him out.

17

Dave squints.

His mother reaches over the seat of the station wagon. "Here, Dave, you look uncomfortable—wear Dad's sunglasses."

He puts them on.

"How's your arm?" his mother asks.

"All right."

"Are you sure you feel well enough—?"

His dad stops for a light. "They want to see him now, Mary. He'll be all right. Mr. Krim's meeting us outside, Dave. I don't know a better lawyer."

"He's known us for years," his mother says. "He sent you a savings bond when you were born."

Dave watches the light change from dark red to dark green.

His dad steps on the gas. His mother's voice sounds strangled. "They'll be decent to him, won't they? One of them is the youth officer. Do you know him, Dave—a man named Enders?"

Dave nods distractedly. "He nabbed Jepson once."

His dad glances awkwardly over his shoulder. "We—we spoke to Jep's mother a little while ago."

"No, please don't," Dave's mom says. "Don't talk about it now, please."

Dave stares out the window. "Where's my car?" he suddenly asks.

"It's been impounded. They have to keep it locked up until the investigation is over."

"Then what?"

"I'm not sure," his dad says. "I think it will have to be scrapped."

Dave sits very still. He's got to collect himself. "What day is today?" he asks them.

His mother whirls around. "Friday. Are you sure—?"

"Mary, they're expecting us *now.*"

Friday, Dave thinks. He's got to speak to Jep before work. Where are they taking him? His dad turns in at the municipal building, parks the car, and gets out.

"Come on, Dave, Larry's waiting for us. That's him over there."

Dave walks in the sun now, Krim's huge hand on his shoulder. He would like to shove it off, but his parents dig this guy. Dave remembers him—how could he not? Six feet six, a real giant. Krim speaks in a low voice as they go through a set of doors. Leading them past a Police Department sign, he guides Dave into a small room, bare except for table and chair. "We've got a little time before they're ready for us. How're you feeling, Dave? I'm sorry to see you in these circumstances. You're a man since I saw you last." Krim offers him a chair. "Would you like to take those sunglasses off?"

"No, thanks," Dave says.

Krim forces a smile. "Well, for now keep them on, then." He pulls out three more chairs. "How's that daughter of yours?" he asks Dave's dad. "Still as full of it as ever?"

"Yeah, I'm afraid she is."

Dave's mother sits down and shields her eyes with her hand.

"Now then." Krim takes out a legal pad and pen. Putting on his glasses, he focuses on Dave. "It's been rough, huh? I can see it has. Tell me what you remember."

Dave hesitates. "Starting when?"

"You were leaving a party, I understand. Taking your friends home."

"Not exactly a party."

"Well, you were over at a friend's house. And you weren't drinking, which is good. Your friend Paul was, though. So what did he do, ask you to take him home?"

"No—"

"Dave," his mom says, "why didn't you wait for the rain to stop? I'm sorry." She covers her face. "I'm sorry, go on."

Krim waits a second. "Your friend Paul got soused and you took care of him. You were being the Good Samaritan. You got in the car—take the story from there."

Dave stares at the big college ring on Krim's right hand.

"Who was sitting where?" Krim asks. "Tell me about that. Your girl friend—"

"She's not!" Dave says.

"Your friend," Krim corrects himself. "She was sitting in the back?"

"Yeah, she came with Jep. He told her to wait there."

"So she was Paul's date—this Susan?"

"Sort of. She came with him."

"And you had nothing to drink."

"No."

Krim looks at Dave's parents. "How's that for irony?

The sober kid who's doing a favor for his friend has *this* happen to him." He scribbles on his pad. "Tell me about the road."

Behind the dark glasses Dave shuts his eyes. What do they want from him?

"The road was slick?" Krim suggests.

"Yeah," Dave says. "Muddy." No, that was later.

"Muddy. We'll look for erosion in that spot. That could be the town's fault."

Dave blinks.

"Dave, how fast were you driving?" Krim asks.

He thinks. "I'm not sure."

"They may know when they inspect the car. About what would you say it was? Over forty? Forty-five?"

"I don't think so. I'm not sure. I was looking in the mirror."

"Someone was behind you?"

Dave is sweating. "Susan."

"I mean some other *car?*"

"No."

Krim's big frame shifting makes the chair creak. "That's what I thought. Your parents said there were no other witnesses." He looks up at them now. "The police talked to the girl last night. I'll see her and her parents later. She was perfectly all right, you said?"

Dave's dad nods.

Krim shakes his head. "It's tragic about the boy—Paul. The lieutenant said it was a freak thing."

Dave feels sweat trickling down his neck.

Krim gives him a nod. "We realize what you're going through. We'll do everything we can. The way I see it, you're the victim almost as much as your friend was. You

were being the good guy and you had some bad luck.
When they question you in a few minutes, answer what
they ask but don't volunteer anything. Harrison Avenue is
known for that curve. Your car was inspected, right?"

"He just had it fixed!" his mother says.

His dad takes her hand. "Come on, Mary. *Dave's* holding up fine—"

A cop with red hair comes into the room and goes over
to Krim now. They all get up at Krim's signal and follow
the cop. Krim lifts off Dave's sunglasses as they walk down
the hall.

"No previous points on your license?"

"No, sir," Dave says.

"What speed were you doing?" the redheaded cop asks.

Krim interrupts. "He told you already."

"I'd like to hear it again, counselor."

"Not over the speed limit, I don't think. The car skid-
ded," Dave says haltingly.

"Is there anything else you can tell us about last night?"

Don't volunteer, Krim just told him. "No." What time
is it? he wonders. He looks at the clock. "I'll be late for
work," he whispers to his dad.

"I spoke to Fred, Dave. You don't have to go in today."

Something is buzzing in Dave's ear now. And it's hot as
hell in here. He'd love to be out somewhere, driving.
Good, they're leaving him out of this. Terrific. They're
leaving, *period.* Nothing he wants more than to get out of
this place.

Back in the station wagon Dave sits in the rear seat again.
He puts on the dark glasses and keeps his head down.

"They seemed sympathetic," his mom says to his dad. "What did you think?"

"I agree." His dad starts the car. "I thought they were fair. They come down hard on the kids who are driving drunk these days, but they saw right away liquor wasn't involved."

"Do they always have to take this to the district attorney?"

"When there's a fatality."

His mom muffles a sound. "I can't believe—" She breaks off. "When will we hear from the D.A.?"

"Whether he's cleared? A couple of weeks at least."

His mom turns around. "How are you feeling, Dave?"

He sits like a zombie.

"Are you hungry?"

"Shall I stop somewhere?" his dad asks.

Dave shakes his head.

"Tell us what we can do for you," his mom begs.

He has a momentary sick urge to laugh, but instead his eyes spill over. What happened is just hitting him. Jep is dead and they're sitting here asking what they can do for *him*.

18

Dave's face is pressed into the pillow, which is damp with perspiration. How long has he been here, stretched out on his bed? They made him sit with them at dinner even though he didn't eat. They made him take off his sunglasses. Can't they leave him alone?

The room is stinking hot but he couldn't care less. Taking the pillow, he covers his face up. Oh, God. If Susan hadn't led him on . . . if she hadn't come that night . . . no, wait, if Jep hadn't been drinking . . . if he'd come by himself. Bullshit!

Dave clenches his hands. It's *his* fault, no one else's. He was trying to see her face. He's not sure if he was speeding, but it's almost beside the point. He should've stayed away from Susan. Like his mom thought at the beginning, *he shouldn't have bought a car.*

Why him, though? He was careful, especially compared to Jep. He never got a ticket, and he even used seat belts sometimes. Why the hell didn't he strap Jepson in that one night? If he had it to do over—hell, if he had it to do over he'd *walk* his whole life! He hears a tap at the door.

"Dave, can I come in?" Lisa asks.

"Not right now. I'm doing something."

"Later?"

"Maybe," he says. But he doubts he'll want to see her. If he lets her in, she'll talk and say it wasn't his fault. Meanwhile Jep's dead, dead like this. Dave clamps the pillow over his face. Now what? He hears footsteps, another knock on his bedroom door.

"Dave?"

It's his father.

"There's someone to see you. Do you want to come down?"

"No!" He tries to be calmer. "No, not right now."

"It's Bob Willoughby. He'd like to see you. Should I have him come up?"

"Not now, Dad." Dave sinks back. "I'm sleeping. Tell him thanks."

"It's still early, nine o'clock—"

"I'm sleeping, Dad, please."

"I'll see if he can come back in the morning."

Dave holds his breath. Maybe if he holds it long enough—no, you pass out and breathe involuntarily. You can't off yourself that way, he remembers from health class. For a second he thinks of something that has nothing to do with the accident, but then he remembers again and buries his head.

He's drifting off to sleep, finally. Please let it be for the whole night. Hey, there's Jep at the foot of the bed. "Hey, man!" Dave says. "I *knew* you weren't really— What are you doing here? Hey, where are you going?" And the next thing he knows Jepson is gone.

The hardest is waking up and having it hit all over again. He's lying on the couch now—what is it, Saturday afternoon? Two days he's gotten through. His arm feels kind of numb. Good. It would serve him right if he was crippled for life.

"How about some ice cream, Dave?"

"No, thanks." His mom's still bugging him to eat something. They're treating him like he's sick. And he is, in a way. Nothing interests him. He aches. There's a golf match on TV now, but the announcer's whispery voice is driving him nuts. The only thing half bearable is being asleep.

Dave rolls over on the couch, his face turned toward the wall. The doorbell rings, his mother goes to the door, he can hear her talking in the hall. If it's Willo again he'll have to see him. How long can he keep saying no?

"Dave?" his mother calls. "Dave, could you please—?"

He hoists himself up.

"It's Pastor Deaner, Dave."

He forces himself to nod as she leads in the minister, and he watches him sit down on the opposite end of the couch. Who is this guy? Dave hardly knows him. He wishes he would go away. His mom turns off the TV and leaves the two of them alone.

"I'm sorry about what happened, Dave," Deaner says, his hands resting on his knees. "Your mother explained to me, and I thought maybe there was something I could do to help."

Dave studies him in silence. Skinny, middle-aged, deep voiced. Help? Sure, bring Jep back. "No, thanks," he says.

"I won't stay long," Deaner tells him. "I think a lot of your parents. Your mother comes to church—"

But not me, is that the point? If he'd gone, Dave wonders suddenly, would things still be normal now?

"It's hard to know why these things happen—"

Dave's mind begins to blur.

"We sometimes wonder if God is there . . ." Pastor Deaner keeps on talking. ". . . hard to comprehend . . ."

It hits Dave at this point what Susan said before the car flew. *He's more exciting than you are—don't kid yourself.* She was right.

Deaner takes a pamphlet from an inside pocket. "Remember how God tested Job?"

Dave isn't listening. He's remembering what happened next in the car. He tried to see her expression and the car took off on its own.

"Dave," Pastor Deaner thumbs the pamphlet—"is there anything you'd like to tell me?"

Yeah, *I'm not worth your time* . . . but he keeps his mouth shut.

"I understand the road conditions were bad. . . ."

Tell him: It was all my fault!

"I'm going to leave this," Deaner says. He lays the pamphlet on the couch.

Dave glances idly at the title: *When God Puts Us to the Test. . . .*

"I'll come and see you soon again. Try not to be too hard on yourself." Deaner shakes Dave's hand and goes.

Dave can hear him speaking to his mother in the hall. She'll come back and want to know how he feels. So Dave does what he's been doing for the last two days—shuts his eyes and pretends to be asleep.

Alone in his room again. Still Sunday, is it possible? At least it's night now. Will hours creep like this for the rest of his life? Hard seeing Willo for the first time—hard seeing the coach, too. Everybody says it could have happened to them. Tears sting his eyes. What do they know?

"Dave?"

Damn, it's Lisa. He shuts his eyes tightly.

She opens the door. "Are you awake, Dave?"

He keeps faking as usual. She waits for a minute and then goes away. He has the urge to bring her back and find out what Susan said. Susan called this afternoon when he really was asleep. His parents keep saying he should call her back, but he can't make himself do it. Maybe he'll lie and tell them he called.

Dave is half conscious. What time is it? He's been dreaming about Jep again when the door of his room opens. This time it's his dad.

"I have something to tell you."

"Yeah?"

"I just spoke to Mrs. Jepson. In the morning there's going to be a private service at the cemetery. There's going to be a memorial later. Do you think you'd like to go to it? The private one, I mean. Just her family, no other friends. She says it's all right for us to come, but you don't have to go."

Dave stares at the ceiling. "Yeah, I want to go."

19

Sunlight comes in through the blinds and makes bars on the bathroom wall. Nicking himself with his razor, Dave lets the drop of blood stay. Then he goes to his room and puts on his shirt. His dad's shirt, that is—he doesn't have one that fits right. With great concentration he knots the tie around his neck. He's feeling strange, like he did at the police station—when was it, days ago? They keep asking if he's sure that he really wants to go.

"Ready, Dave?"

"Yeah." He ties his shoes and comes downstairs. The shoes are still a little stiff from being hosed the night Jep threw up.

"Nice." His mother wets her forefinger and wipes the blood off his cheek.

Dave's dad edges toward the door. "Okay, let's go."

Lisa comes in from the kitchen. "I want to go too, Mom and Dad. I think—"

Her dad shakes his head. "We'd like you to stay."

"I want to be with Dave! I want him to know I feel as bad as he does!"

"He knows that," her mother says. She hugs Lisa and then they leave.

Sitting in the back of the station wagon, Dave finds everything unreal. Belle Park seems like a movie set or a place from long ago. He looks out the window, relieved that his parents aren't talking. At Mount Saint Matthew's Cemetery his dad slows down and makes a left. Inside the gates his father follows a serpentine. They pass some moss-covered stones and drive up a hill. They've always come here before to visit the grave of Dave's grandparents. For a minute he's confused. Is this Memorial Day?

He doesn't remember getting out of the station wagon, but suddenly he's on a hilltop, standing between his mom and dad. A minister is already there. A little way behind him Dave sees a green tent. Beneath the tent is a mound of dirt. Now more people are coming—three, no four of them. One is Jep's mom, whom Dave hasn't seen in a while. He should probably say hello, but she isn't looking his way. With her is a woman who must be Jep's aunt. On the other side of Jep's mom is a man Dave doesn't recognize. The fourth person—from the funeral home?—tells the minister to start.

Dave can't hear so well, but it isn't the minister's fault—more like something is clogging his ears and his head. His mom takes his hand now, as if he's a little kid, and his dad puts an arm around him. The minister speaks.

"A time to mourn, and a time to dance . . . a time to embrace, and a time to refrain from embracing. . . ." Sounds like a song the Byrds did a long time ago. Words from the Bible? The Bible snaps shut and the minister goes on talking. Dave tries to listen, but it's no use, he can't.

"In the name of the Father . . ."

The prayer's almost over. Dave feels his mom and his dad start to stir. There's a sob from Jep's aunt as the coffin goes into the ground. Jep's mom tosses a flower on top of it. Dave hears ". . . *forever, amen.*"

The minister takes Jep's mom's arm, and they all turn

toward Dave now. He feels dizzy—they're looking at him.

"Thank you for coming," Mrs. Jepson says. "This is my sister, and Paul Jepson, Senior, my former husband, Jep's father...."

Dave stares at the dark mustache and curly hair, and his knees start to give way. He feels himself going until somebody—his dad?—catches him and holds him as he starts to sink down.

20

Dave pushes another copper strip into a plastic flashlight cylinder, like he's been doing all day every day for the last couple of weeks. He's not sorry that his dad made him come back here the day after the funeral. He'd have gone out of his head by now, sitting home on the couch. Not that he's in such great shape when he comes in to work, but at least his hands are busy and his parents get a break. It's hard enough for them when he's home in the evenings, trying to make conversation and go on with their lives.

Work isn't bad. He can do his job blind. Even now he's poking in the copper strip while he looks across the room. He minds his own business, though. The women assemblers feel sorry for him. He sees them glance in his direction and then whisper to each other. It's even harder facing people outside of work, though. His old friends who knew Jep don't know what to say. The cops have finished investigating and Mrs. Jepson isn't going to sue, but instead of feeling better Dave feels more weighted down.

"What did Susan tell the cops?" he asked Krim while the investigation was on.

"That you were one of the best drivers of anyone your age."

Is that all? He almost wishes she'd mentioned their

fight in the car. It's still bothering him, the fact that he's kept that to himself. Should he go back to the cops? He would, except for his parents. If he keeps this thing going it'll get them upset. He's thought of calling up Susan, but what would he say to her? She hasn't called him again, and he's grateful for that. There are other people he'd like to talk to, but he hasn't found the nerve for it. He'd like to ask Dr. Kraft exactly what killed Jep. If he'd gotten him out of the car, would it have made any difference? Was it quick or was it painful?—depressing things like that.

"Five-thirty," Staller calls out. "You can go, Dave. Time to quit."

Dave, glancing up, sees that everyone else has gone. He finishes his last assembly, wipes his face on his shirt sleeve, and walks down the aisle as the main lights go off.

"Don't you want this?" At the door Staller hands him an envelope.

"Oh. Yeah," Dave says. "Thanks." He forgot it's payday.

Staller pauses uncertainly. "How're things going?"

"Okay, thanks."

"Can I give you a lift?"

"No, thanks." Dave keeps moving. Staller, nodding, doesn't push it, and Dave is glad he gives up. It's so awkward making small talk. Besides, he doesn't mind walking the two miles home. It's the one time he lets himself daydream as he walks. The first thing he daydreams is *the accident never happened.* He pictures himself as he was this time last year. Then, next, he dreams ahead, where he's older and in a new life.

As soon as Dave reaches his own street, he forces himself to quit daydreaming altogether. He usually goes into the house through the garage, where his car used to be. No one has told him what happened to it and he hasn't asked. On the way in he sees the oil stain that it made on the floor.

Tonight as he comes in he feels sick from the oil smell. Damn, they're ready to eat and Lisa's not here. He hates to admit it, but it's better when Lisa's around. With her putting in her two cents there's less burden on him.

"Hi, Dave."

"Hi," he says. His mom looks almost cheerful. "Where's Lisa?" he asks.

"She's eating at McDonald's with Pam and Patrice."

Dave washes his hands and sits down at the table.

His dad is there waiting. "How goes it?" he asks.

Lately everything his dad says sounds awkward. "It goes okay."

"Glad to hear it." His dad smiles and leans on the table. "Good news. The district attorney's office called this afternoon. They've cleared you. There won't be a trial. You're okay."

"Isn't it wonderful?" his mom says. "We were confident all along, but to have it be official is an enormous relief." She puts her hands on the back of his chair. "As soon as I heard, I went over to church. Maybe you'll want to do that, too."

"They aren't going to ask me anything else?"

"It's over." His dad sits back. "They aren't suspending your license. There was no evidence they could find that you did anything wrong. Larry says the D.A. is recommending that the road be redesigned. Maybe you'd like to write Larry Krim thanking him for all he's done."

Dave stares in silence at the plate that's in front of him.

"I thought we'd celebrate with a steak," his mom says. "Here, have some sauce."

Dave watches them and forces himself to imitate what they're doing. The first piece of steak feels as if it is stuck in his throat.

His dad, studying him, puts his fork down. "Wait a minute. Here we're saying it's over and you're thinking oh, no, no."

Dave clears his throat.

"I thought so. Look, we know—"

His mom shuts her eyes. "Don't think that we'll ever forget Jep! Not an hour goes by that we don't wish—" Her voice cracks. "But we have to start *somewhere* going on with our lives."

Dave's dad grabs her hand across the table. "Mom's right. Today isn't a bad day to try and make the start. It's good news from the D.A. *We* knew it, but now everybody does. You're clear, and we hope you'll start seeing your friends again."

"Maybe begin to look at colleges," his mother says quietly.

His dad nods. "And there's football. How about that?"

"Football?" Dave says. "What about it?"

"I saw your coach at the bowling alley. He's dying to have you come out for the team."

Dying. Dave sees his dad flush. A lot of ordinary words are loaded now.

"I'd be happy about it, too, if you decided to play." His mother gets up and goes over to the stove. "You know I wasn't enthusiastic when you went out in ninth grade. Now I'd love to see you involved in something again."

Dave toys with his steak. He's given them such a rough

time of it. Maybe he should go out for football just to give them a break.

"Another thing," his mom says as she comes back to the table. "We've decided to go to North Carolina Labor Day weekend. Would you like to come along with us? You could relax and play some golf."

"Is Lisa going?" Dave asks.

"No, she's going away with Pam's family."

That means a whole weekend of just him and them. "If I went out for football, I'd have to go to football camp then."

"Oh, go *there,* no question." His dad is all smiles.

"Yes." His mom laughs. "I'm sure you'd rather be with friends. Oh, wait." She gets up. "Something came for you in the mail today. I'll get it. Stay here."

She returns with an envelope. Then she sits down and watches him, hoping he'll open it. But he won't, not in front of them. His mom tries to be casual. "Is it from Susan?"

"No, it isn't." From Nan. He can tell from the neat printing. He's almost forgotten about her, like he's forgotten everyone. By this time he's managed to slip a piece of steak into his napkin so he won't have to force it down. He gets up from the table. "Excuse me, okay?"

"You're excused," his mom says.

He can tell she's feeling relieved because somebody his age still remembers him.

Dave sits at his desk with his head in his arms. Pressing on his eyelids, he sees circles of purple and black. If he could just *not be here anymore,* instead of faking going on with his life . . . He raises his hand to his head and wipes off the sweat. The evening is the worst time. He's tried a couple of things, including the Bible, but the last psalm he read was about sinking in mire. One thing he has read is *The Great Gatsby,* the book from English class. Somehow he got to thinking that Gatsby reminds him of Jep. There's an automobile accident in the story, caused by somebody being careless. Dave's upset by the scene but he rereads it anyway.

Tonight, though, he doesn't feel like reading anything. He stumbles off the desk chair and onto his bed. Go to sleep, go to work, when September comes play football. Go through motions forever and try to turn off his thoughts. He lies on his back, staring up at the beige walls. He knows now he'll never paint them as long as he's here. Eventually he remembers the letter from Nan. He tears open the envelope and reads it in the dark.

Dear Dave,

I've been thinking about you a lot. I guess you haven't wanted to talk or maybe you'd have called. If it's easier to write, I'd be glad to hear from you that way. Meanwhile, take care.

Sincerely,
Nan

Nice of her, Dave thinks, as he lets the note fall to the floor. Everybody's nice to him—he wishes they weren't. Writing would be easier than facing someone in person, but the least pain of all is keeping strictly to himself.

21

"We're going to miss you, Dave." Staller gets up from his desk.

Dave walks into the office. "My last day, Mr. Staller. I just wanted to say good-bye."

"Good luck to you, Dave. You've been real steady all summer. I can't remember hiring a young guy more reliable than you." Staller thrusts out his hand. "It's been a real pleasure. I told your dad we'd keep you on part time, but he says you're going to play ball. I'm glad to hear that."

Dave shakes Staller's hand.

"Going to put on a few pounds?" Smiling, Staller looks at Dave's waist.

"I'll try to."

"Good enough," Staller says. "I sure wish you luck. And I just want to say"—he lets go of Dave's hand now—"I think you've handled this problem of yours like a man."

"Thanks." Dave keeps his face blank. He's good at that these days. He's even getting so he's able to look people in the eye. Let the conversation end, though, Dave thinks. Good. Staller's taking out the pay envelope.

"You'll find a little something extra in there," Staller says. "I like to give a cash bonus when a man's done consistent work. Put it away for college." He smiles. "Like hell you will, right?"

"Thanks a lot," Dave says. "I don't know what I'd have done if it wasn't for coming here—" He breaks off. "I'll be back for a visit sometime."

Staller steers him to the door. "You do that. Say hi to your dad, okay?"

Dave hurries out the front way to avoid seeing the parking lot. The spot where he used to park with Susan still gives him the creeps. This is it, then, the last time he'll walk home from this place. The blast of a car horn takes him by surprise.

"Jacoby, over here!" Willo calls from his car.

No way to get by him—he's parked by the curb. Dave prepares his face carefully. "What are you doing here?"

Willo breaks into a smile. "Thought I'd pick you up, man, on your last day of work."

"Thanks, but I'm going somewhere."

"Where? I'll drop you off."

Dave comes closer. He could tell Willo, but he'd rather be cool. "I've got to stop off somewhere—"

"I'll take you," Willo insists.

Dave hesitates and then gets into Willo's old car. Seat lumpy, funny smell. Strange to be sitting here after all this time. Easier to go along than to argue the point. He'll make up a destination. "I'm just going a few blocks."

"In a hurry?" Willo asks.

"Sort of. Well, no *big* rush."

"Good." Willo shuts off the motor and smiles again shyly. "I've been trying to track you down since you signed up for the football team. I'm really glad you're going out. I'm looking forward to it."

Dave nods distractedly. "My dad thought I should."

"Your dad?" Willo shifts. "What about you?"

"I think I should too."

"You don't sound convinced." Willo squeezes the steering wheel. "Your dad's making you play—is that how it is?"

Dave shakes his head. "Not *making* me. I'm hoping I'll get into it once I'm out there."

"You're still—" Willo substitutes a long sigh for words.

"Yeah," Dave admits. "It's not getting any better."

Willo's gray eyes avoid him and then meet his straight on. "A few times I've been thinking, and I put myself in your shoes. I picture me, you know, driving my car, and something like that happening— I'm telling you, I don't know what I'd do. This thing you're going through must be pure hell. Especially since you loved the guy." Willo's face flushes. "You know what I mean, were best friends, whatever."

Dave shuts his eyes.

"What a nut—Jep," Willo goes on. "I've been thinking about him a lot lately. Did you know that I found his Moped in my garage? I called up his mom and she said I should keep it. It works good, but I don't know. When I see it, I *think*."

Dave clears his throat. "How's she doing?"

"Jep's mom? I couldn't tell. She didn't say much. I guess it takes a lot of time." Willo squeezes the wheel again. "I heard you're all clear. I guess the worst hell would be having it be your fault."

Dave sits still.

Willo notices his expression. "Hey, I'm shooting my mouth off. I didn't mean to get into this. Want a ride to camp tomorrow?"

Dave breathes uneasily. "I guess so. What time are you going?"

"Nine, I'll pick you up. Will your dad be coming by to watch?"

"No, my parents are going golfing for the weekend."

"Nice deal. I wouldn't mind that."

"I could have gone," Dave says.

Willo, brightening, starts the engine. "But you didn't want to miss camp. How much do you want to bet you'll be glad you came out? Let's go, okay? Where're you headed?"

"Toward your house. Go on. I'll show you when we get there."

"Man of mystery, huh?" The car rolls down the street. "Have you seen anyone?"

"Not really."

"How about Susan?"

"No."

"I haven't either. I heard she's out of town. Four more days and school starts. Can you believe *senior year?*" Willo steps on the gas and turns right at the corner. "Listen, Dave, and don't say no until I finish. I'm having a few people over to my house tonight. I'd like—"

"I don't think so."

"Let me finish! A few friends from the team are coming over. And a couple of girls. We'll be breaking up early because of training tomorrow. No booze, even. Really low key. Come on, what do you say?"

Dave nods out the window at the record store on the corner. "This is where I'm going. Let me off here, okay?"

"Will you come over tonight?" Willo moves into the right lane.

"Okay, for a while." Dave gets out of the car.

"About eight," Willo calls as he pulls away from the curb.

Dave waits until Willo has blended in with the traffic before he begins walking quickly away from the stores. He doesn't have much time if he wants to make it home for dinner, but he's got to stop off—it'll be a few days until he can come again. Crossing at Franklin Street, he passes the last few shops and goes on by the park in the direction of Mount Saint Matthew's.

Is that—? He looks ahead of him. Lately he's been walking with his head down. Yeah, it is—Nan. He wouldn't mind seeing her, except that he never answered that note she sent. If he slows up a little she'll be gone and that'll be that. Something, though, makes him speed up and he calls her. "Hey, Nan!"

"Dave!" She turns around and smiles. "So strange, I was just thinking about you. Did you ever get—?"

"Yeah, I got it." He falls into step with her. "Thanks. I started to write you, but I couldn't. I wish I had." She's watching him, he sees, but not with a pitying look. "Where're you going?" he asks.

"Home. I just got off work."

He notices she's wearing jeans and an old denim shirt. "Where do you work?"

"At the Belle Park Animal Shelter. I clean out the cages."

"No shit." Sounds like a Jepson remark.

Nan laughs. "There's a lot of it, as a matter of fact. If there weren't, I guess I'd be out of a job." They walk on in silence for a few seconds. "Are you still working?"

"Today was my last day," he says.

"Are you glad?"

"I'm not sure. I guess so. I'm not ready to go back to school."

"I'm not either," she says.

"Just the normal reasons?"

Nan sighs and shifts her bag to the other arm. "No. Compared to what you're going through, this sounds like nothing, I guess. But it's hard, really confusing. I'm having this problem with my father."

"What is it?"

Nan stops on the corner. "Do you have time to talk for a minute? This is where I usually turn."

"Yeah, let's sit down," Dave says, and they walk over to a bench near the park.

Nan sits at one end. "I feel stupid making a big thing of this. You obviously have enough on your mind as it is."

"Tell me."

Nan plays with her bag. "Thanks. I don't have anyone to talk to, really. I write letters to Jane, but she's three thousand miles away. I can usually call my mother, but not about this." Nan takes a breath. "My father met this woman. I came East, I think I told you, mainly because he wanted 'his share of me,' as he said. Now it seems"—her voice breaks—"he wants Gloria to move in." Nan smiles ruefully. "Isn't it a weird situation? And the worst of it is, he's leaving the decision about it completely up to me."

"*You* decide whether this Gloria moves into your house or not?"

"Yes! How can I win? If I say no, I'm being selfish, and if I say yes and it's awful, that'll be my fault, too!" Nan adjusts the barrette at the end of her braid. "And he has to know quickly because of her apartment lease or something. I have to make up my mind before school starts next week."

"What are you going to tell him?"

"I don't know. I'll say one thing, she's the complete opposite of my mother." Nan rolls her eyes. "She can't cook worth a damn. She'a always sending out for Chinese food. I like Chinese food, or I used to, at least. Gloria talks baby talk to my father and she's very into *labels*."

Dave nods. "I get the picture. She sounds like Susan Scherra a couple of years from now."

Nan looks at him cautiously. "Have you seen Susan at all?"

"No."

She runs a finger over the rough wood of the bench. "You don't want to?"

"No. If it were up to me I'd never see her again."

"Why, because it would remind you—?"

"Not just that. *Everything* reminds me." Dave squirms uncomfortably and slouches down on the bench. "Harrison Street reminds me, Jep's apartment, when I pass it. The school, cars, guitars, beer . . . breathing *the air in Belle Park*. With Susan it's more than just reminding." He grinds his heel under the bench. "It's her knowing certain things that no one else knows."

Nan waits a second for him to go on. "I'm not sure what you mean. What kind of things?"

He's sweating all of a sudden. "Forget it. I'm not sure myself. Maybe I'll take you up on writing a letter—get it straight in my head that way." He glances at his watch. "I'd better be going. I'm stopping by the cemetery."

Nan gets up first. "Do you go there often?"

"Every day for a while now." Dave rises. "Does it sound morbid?"

"No, it sounds right. That's what cemeteries are for."

Dave hesitates, hands in pockets. "It's not like I think he knows I'm there, or anything."

Nan meets his eyes. "But *you* know."

"It's all I can do." Dave shrugs. "The only thing I can think of. I feel better when I go. I don't even know why." He backs away from the bench. "You're not in a hurry?"

"Not really. My father's away."

Shifting his weight, Dave wipes his forehead. "Feel like going over there with me? Unless it's too far . . ."

"No, I'd like to," Nan says. They cross the street and walk without saying much the rest of the way to Mount Saint Matthew's.

"It's gotten flatter." Dave nods at the mound.

"There's no tombstone yet?"

"Just that temporary thing." Dave motions to Nan and they sit on the grass. "At first I used to stand," he says, "like it was disrespectful to sit down or something. Then I figured I ought to be as natural as I can. What do you think?"

"I agree." Nan tucks her knees under her. "I used to hate cemeteries, especially certain ones in California, you know? I can see though how this, here, could actually help you feel at peace—the people who come here to visit, I mean. What do you think about when you come here?"

"The nicer stuff, mostly. How we used to sit in his room, hacking around after school. Know what I think about?" Dave pulls a blade of grass. "One time I asked him, 'Aren't you afraid even of dying?' And he said, 'Why should I be?' What could be so bad about *tasting it,* as he called it, and spending eternity with Morrison and Hendrix?"

"Maybe that's what he's doing."

"I keep hoping," Dave says.

They walk down from the top of the hill and come out through the cemetery gates.

"Are you serious about writing to me?" Nan asks as she's about to go on her way.

"Yeah, I am," Dave says. "Not tonight though. I told Willougby I'd stop by."

"Really?" She smiles. "He asked me to come, too. So I'll see you over there. What did he say, around eight?"

"Yeah. I'd better be getting home to dinner." Dave slowly backs away. "Thanks for coming with me just now. It's like I have to get used to people all over again."

"I felt comfortable being there."

"So did I. See you later."

22

"So long." Dave stands in the hallway and looks into the living room.

"You're going out?" His mother bolts out of her chair.

"Just for a little while, over to Willo's house."

His dad drops the newspaper. "Want to use the car?"

"No, thanks, I feel like walking."

"Okay, we'll leave the light on for you."

"I'll be home pretty early," he says. "I have to get out my stuff for football camp."

"We have to finish packing too." His mother is in the hall now. "We're hoping to get off by eight. How about you?"

"Willo's picking me up about nine."

"Have a good time tonight." His mom stands by the door.

"Yeah," he says awkwardly. She's making a big deal of this. She's happy he's going out, but sort of nervous, too.

"Are you sure you don't want to change your mind and come with us tomorrow?" she asks.

"To North Carolina? No Mom, come on."

"I just thought—" She rubs her arms as if there's a breeze. "I just thought you might enjoy it better than camp."

"Mary!" His dad gets up. "They're counting on him.

You're acting like he's two years old and you can't leave him out of your sight!"

"Sorry." She steps back. "I guess I've been working with kids that age too long. Go on. We'll see you in the morning."

"Enjoy yourself," his dad says.

Dave hates to admit it, but he's more nervous than his mom is, as he walks down the street and crosses at the light. This is the first time he'll be seeing a bunch of friends all at once. With Nan there it may be easier. Still, he feels tense. Willo's street is coming up. Dave slows to a shuffle. He can't help thinking this is where all his troubles began. If Jep had come alone that night— Quit it, he tells himself. He's got to forget *ifs* and face how it is.

"Jacoby!" Willo calls from the porch. He slaps Dave's palm noisily. "The others are in the back. Come on, through the house. I swear we're so straight tonight, I feel like I ought to be serving animal crackers."

"Who's here?" Dave asks.

"Tommy and Sandy. Bill . . . Nan Tobin. She said she saw you today. Mazur's coming over later." Willo leads him through the kitchen, where he gets him a Coke. "Ready for tomorrow?"

"As ready as I'll ever be."

"Go on out back. I'll be there in a second."

Dave goes out onto the patio, where everyone is sitting around a table. Sandy, Tom, Bill, and Nan are drinking sodas and playing cards. They all look up at him.

Nan smiles. "Hi."

"Hi." Dave nods.

Tom motions him over. "Hi, Jacoby. Me and Bill are just finishing a hand."

Bill belches. "All I am as a card freak I owe to my

grandma. She started me on go fish when I was three years old."

"How's it going, Jacoby?" Tom asks casually.

"Not too bad," Dave says, sitting next to Nan.

Bill riffles his cards. "Ready for basic training tomorrow?"

Dave shrugs. "Yeah. I hear it's going to be hot as hell."

"I think I'll open a Gatorade stand," Nan says.

"Four whole days and nights you're there?" Sandy asks.

"Yep." Bill shuffles his cards again. "The point is to cement us together."

"Don't knock team unity!" Willo appears with a can of potato chips. "Hey, you guys hear something? I think I hear somebody coming."

"Mazur, maybe," Bill says. "His car sounds like a bull-dozer."

"I'm checking it out." Willo heads around toward the front of the house.

"Check 'em, Willo!" Bill calls. "Don't let no riffraff in!"

"You two don't mind if we finish playing this hand?" Bill asks to Dave and Nan.

"Go head." Dave turns to Nan. "Feel like taking a walk?"

"Sure."

"Tell Willo we'll be right back." They get up from the table. Walking along the row of bushes that marks the boundary of Willo's yard, they pass in front of the open garage, and Dave comes to a stop. On the right against the wall is Jep's Moped, where he left it. "Wait," Dave says. He looks at it. "That was his—that was Jep's." Key still in the ignition. Sand clinging to the spokes. "Come on, let's get out of here." He pulls Nan away. *Quit thinking,* he tells himself. "What did you have for dinner?" he asks with forced lightness. "Fried rice and egg foo yong?"

"Not tonight." Nan laughs. "I told you my father was out. Maybe he took her *out* for Chinese food." They enter an alleyway. Nan watches his face. "How are you doing?"

"So-so."

"The Moped's one more reminder, isn't it?"

He nods.

"You miss him a lot."

"Yeah, yeah I do." Coming out on a side street, Dave meanders farther. "We were planning this trip, Jep and I. We'd be out there right now."

"Where?"

"End of the Island—Montauk Point. Ever been there?"

"Yes, my father took me once when we first came."

"Jep and I were going to go out around now, when we finished our jobs. We were going to camp out in this great spot that's always so private because you can only get there by climbing down this sort of a cliff. Last year we went by train and hitched out to Montauk Point. We had such a great time swimming. We stayed for three days. This year we would have— Jesus." He stops. "I can't talk about it, I really can't."

Nan waits for a second. "It seems like it helps you to tell me things—but don't worry, take your time with it. You must be tired of people telling you that time heals everything."

Dave, nodding, starts walking again. "That doesn't include you."

"Good. I wish I could help more."

"You're helping, believe me." He turns around toward

Willo's house. "You're the only person so far I feel slightly normal with."

"That may be because we didn't know each other well before. It must be harder for you with everyone else, trying to be good old Dave."

"I guess that's part of it," Dave says. "There's sure nobody else I feel like talking to. So if you have the patience to wait it out . . ."

"I think I do."

"Let's go back to the party. And let's change the subject." Picking a leaf, he hands it to her. "Have you thought any more about Gloria?"

"I'm trying as hard as I can not to tonight." Nan slips the leaf into her buttonhole. "Every time I think about her, I feel like going back to Santa Barbara."

He turns. "You wouldn't, would you?"

"Probably not, but it's occurred to me."

"I hope you don't. What's all that racket?" he asks as they enter Willo's yard.

"More kids, it looks like. You know Willo, can't say no to anybody. Who is it?"

"Bull Curtis." Dave pauses. "I'm going inside to the bathroom. I'll be right back."

"What's happening?" he asks Willo as he passes him in the kitchen.

"I couldn't keep Bull out—not a guy on the team. Where are you going?"

"Upstairs to the can." Climbing the steps, Dave walks down the dark hall. The bathroom door is closed, and underneath he sees a light. Hurry up, he thinks, leaning on the windowsill. Sounds drift up, as he waits, from the patio below.

"Turn the music down!" Willo yells.

Someone does, and Dave hears voices.

"Football camp sucks."

"Yeah. You hear Jacoby's coming out for the team?"

Dave looks down on Mazur and Curtis.

"Yeah. He's here tonight, you know."

"He is? Where?"

"Have you seen him since the accident?"

"Nope," Bull says, yawning. "I hear he looks like a zombie."

"Who told you that?"

"I don't know. Somebody."

"What's he out for, left tackle like you?"

"No, I'm up against Tom." Bull yawns again and the yawn becomes a chuckle. "How about this, Mazur? I get *Jacoby* to drive Tommy home tonight—get it? Tommy at left tackle? That ought to clear the way for me!"

Dave can't tell if Mazur's laughing. Goddamn Curtis, anyway. He should go down there and flatten his face. Instead he's just standing here. Let him into the bathroom! Dave knocks on the door. As it opens he draws back. "Susan." He stiffens.

She smoothes her hair. "I came with Bull."

"Still crashing parties, I see."

"And you still hate me." Her cheeks are flushed. Her voice is controlled, though. "It's strange, you know, Dave? I thought you'd be grateful. I could have messed up the rest of your life by saying certain things."

Dave's mouth is dry. "I didn't want any favors. The rest of my life is messed up anyway."

Susan glowers. "What did you want me to tell the cops, *he was jealous of his best friend?*"

Is she saying he wanted Jep to die? No, she *couldn't* think that.

"I could have told the cops you went wild when I said Jep was better than you." Susan sways in the doorway. Her voice becomes shriller now. "I could have told them you loved me since seventh grade—you *did,* Dave. I could have told them you were acting so mad in the car, but I kept my mouth shut."

"I *wanted* you to tell them," Dave says. He bites his cheeks to keep from losing his cool. "It's driving me nuts that they let me off!"

"Oh, really?" Susan's eyes narrow. "Well, now that I know that, I'll help you out. I have all senior year to spread the details around. It hasn't been easy for me either, you know," she says as her lips twitch. "You dumped me and killed Jepson and now I'm all by myself."

"I didn't *kill* him!" Dave shouts.

Susan pushes past him. "It comes to the same thing," she says, her heels clicking on the stairs.

He starts to follow, then backs off and drifts into the bathroom, where he sees his face in the mirror. *Get out of here now.* He slips down the stairs and out the front door when no one is looking. On the way home he runs first, then slows to a jog.

While he's jogging it comes to him. Suddenly it's clear what he has to do. Luck is with him. When he gets home his parents are in bed. No discussion, no explanations. He goes to his room, where he doesn't sleep, of course. There's too much to figure out. Before long the telephone rings.

"I'll get it," he calls. "It's for me," he tells his parents as they open the bedroom door. Willo believes him when he says he's sick. Nan isn't as gullible.

"You saw Susan Scherra," she says.

"Right. Look, I'm not feeling well. I'll see you after camp. Give me Willo again, please."

"Think you'll be better by tomorrow?" Willo asks.

"Yeah, I'll make sure I am."

"See you at nine. Get some sleep."

"Okay. See you then." Dave returns to his room more convinced than he was before. They won't understand what he's doing, but he can't worry about that.

23

They're leaving. Dave hovers at the curb. He's been going crazy waiting, but suddenly he feels like calling them back. His mother waves and his dad starts the car.

"See you Tuesday!" his mom calls.

"Good luck at camp!" Then his dad pulls out of the driveway and Dave goes inside the house.

He's not completely ready yet, and he only has a few minutes to spare. He stands in a daze in the middle of the living room. God, the couch where he lay so long, wanting to disappear. If things go the way he hopes, he may never see it again. Get moving, he tells himself. Call Willo, first thing. Going to the phone, he clears his throat as he dials.

"Willo?" *Make this good.* "You don't have to come for me. My dad's going to drop me off. He wants to, you know? You ready to leave now? Okay, I'll see you over there." Hanging up the receiver, he leans against the wall. The timing could mess him up. He's got to be careful. He should have tried to find out if Willo's mom is still home.

Get it together. He runs around the house, gathering his camping stuff. Could his parents tell he was nervous? About football camp, they must have thought. The worst was saying good-bye to Lisa—he would have liked to try to explain to her, but she never would have kept quiet.

What else does he need? Flashlight. His wallet with the hundred twenty-five in cash.

Hell, his fingers are all thumbs as he goes through his wallet. Cards fall on the floor—social security, I.D. His driver's license, which several times he has thought of tearing into pieces. But he stuffs everything in again and puts the wallet in his backpack. He wishes like anything he could stop his hands from shaking as he grabs all his things and carts them downstairs. While he stands at the door, a horn beeps, making him hyper. If it's Willo, he'll run out the back. Dave looks out cautiously.

It's someone at the neighbor's house. Dave waits until the car leaves. Then he picks up his gear to see how it feels. He hopes he won't attract attention walking down the street now. The next fifteen minutes or so are going to be tense.

The phone rings. Without thinking he picks it up. His voice comes out strangely. "Hello?"

"Is Dave there?"

He hangs up. Damn, it was Nan. He should have let it ring. Now she'll worry. She may call again. He'd better get going. On impulse he scrawls a few lines on the pad by the phone. *Dear Mom and Dad, I can't take going back to school. I'm heading for California. Please don't try to find me. Don't worry. I'll get a job. I love you and I'll be okay. Dave.*

During the last minutes in the house he feels like taking more things along. Souvenirs. No, don't, it'll be too much weight. He leaves and locks the door. To anyone watching it has to seem like he's going off to football camp. The big thing is to give Willo the slip if he's early and comes this way.

Dave's pulse is pounding like mad when he finally gets

to Willo's street. There's no one around and all the cars are gone. Dave is sure no one's home, but he sneaks up cautiously anyway. The Moped is there as if it's been waiting for him. Tying his sleeping bag to the back of its seat, he considers what to do next. He rolls the Moped silently out of the garage and pushes it up the block. Then, making sure that no nosy neighbor is watching, he fiddles with the key until the engine turns over and starts.

Dave jumps onto the seat, his pack bumping his shoulders, and he heads for the highway. He feels bad about the lie. He had to say California to throw them off track, otherwise they might look for him closer to home. He hangs on to the handlebars. It seems bizarre to be riding this. He feels—this is strange—he feels connected to Jep. Turning onto the service road and then Sunrise Highway, he sees a sign: *95 miles.* He ought to be able to make it by early afternoon.

Dave wipes sweat off his forehead with the sleeve of his T-shirt. On his right stunted pine trees are growing in sand. Cars zip by on his left—Labor Day weekend traffic. It's clouding over now—looks like it's going to rain. Soon he'll pass by the place where his family rented a house once. He breathes deeply, filling his lungs with briny sea air. At the same time, the Moped sputters, bringing him back to reality. This isn't a vacation. This is *his life* from now on.

What time is it, anyway? Four o'clock and still a way to go. He's been on the road since morning, making stops that have taken forever—fixing a gear on the bike, forcing himself to eat something, waiting for road construction to get cleared up. He nudges the Moped now as if it were a pony, but instead of going faster it sputters again. He'd better stop at the gas station coming up on the right. Feeling a first drop of rain, he looks up at the sky. If it rains hard, he'll be tempted to spend money on a room tonight. He'll never get into a campground this late in the day. If he were with someone, they'd sleep out, but by himself— hell, get used to it. That's how it's going to be from now on.

Dave veers to the right as a truck rumbles by him. Some pebbles hit his legs and he curses under his breath. Maybe he shouldn't have come here—he should have gone somewhere else instead. What is he, crazy? On *a hundred twenty-five bucks?* Mainly, it might be easier finding a job here, where he knows his way around a little. Here's the gas station. He slows down and pulls up to the pump.

"Two ounces or three?" The attendant, his own age, smiles at him.

Dave knows he should laugh, but he isn't in the mood. "I'll take care of it myself if you want me to," he says.

"No, that's okay." The attendant nods at the bike. "How fast can you do?"

"About forty-five."

The attendant swings the gas hose around. "You live around here?"

"No—yeah." Dave feels like an idiot. "Summers," he says.

"Where are you from?"

Dave pretends he didn't hear. "How much?" he asks, glancing at the pump.

"Two-fifty. Your back tire's a little low. Want me to put air in it?"

"Yeah, thanks," Dave says. Meanwhile he digs the wallet out of his backpack and hands over three bills.

The attendant takes them and leans down with the air hose. Just then Dave hears a hum and sees a car pulling in. Blue and gold—a state police car. Dave sees the cop getting out of it. He's probably being paranoid, but he can't help himself. "Forget it," he says to the attendant. "I'll fill the tire later." Hurriedly shifting his backpack, he hops on the bike. He bumps across asphalt and heads toward the highway, while the attendant calls after him, "Hey, man, your change!"

"Keep it!" Dave yells.

"Wait!"

But Dave keeps going. No sense hanging around cops. Chugging toward Montauk, he steps harder on the gas. At this point nobody but Willo could have noticed that he's taken off. After Tuesday, though, when his parents get back, then he'll really have to watch out.

A car honks as it passes and Dave lowers his chin to his chest. He's worried about being recognized by somebody from home. It's not very likely, but no sense taking chances. Belle Park is behind him now. He wants to keep it that way.

The wind, blowing up, cools his forehead and arms now. He's kind of glad that the sun is covered by clouds. He sees a sign *State Police*, which makes him speed up even faster. *Come on*, he says to the Moped, like he used to talk to his car. Jep did that, too, talked to the Moped and the Batmobile. So many habits like that that he picked up from Jep.

When the first shower hits him, Dave doesn't mind getting wet himself, but the Moped's getting drenched too, which bothers him more. Soon the rain comes down harder—he can barely see where's he going. Passing cars splash up water and his motor coughs again. Forget it, he decides, he'll go the rest of the way tomorrow. He pulls in at a guest house that has a garage.

"Sorry, we're filled up," a woman calls through the downpour. "Try the motel up there on the left."

Before he goes on, he pulls the poncho out of his backpack. Even with the poncho draped over him, he's soaked to the skin. Pushing on to the motel that the woman pointed out, he parks the Moped under the eaves and goes in out of the rain.

"A single for tonight? You're lucky, I got one left."

"Can I keep my Moped inside?" Dave asks the man at the desk.

"In your room? Well—if you're careful and dry it off good. That'll be thirty-three dollars now."

"Now?"

"That's how we do it. Do you want it or not?"

"I guess so." Dave lifts his pack down and begins rooting around in it. Toilet kit, underwear. What the hell is going on? He ends up dumping everything out on the floor. Towel, extra jeans, toilet kit again. Jesus—it can't be—his wallet is gone.

24

Dave goes through his backpack two or three more times, while the man behind the desk stands there with his arms folded. Then Dave gets up clumsily, feeling like a fool, and says, "I must have lost it down the road. I just paid for gas." The motel man shrugs and, without saying a word, opens the door for him. The rain is pelting down even harder than before. On his way to the Moped, Dave's first thought is to backtrack. The kid at the gas station must have his wallet. Dave gets on the bike, the motor sputters, and he starts out from under the eaves. Before he even hits the highway, though, he changes his mind. He's got *nothing* now, no I.D., no money, a clean slate. He won't go back for his wallet. That way he'll *have* to start a new life.

He buries his chin in his poncho. Cars splash as they whiz by. Thunder rumbles in the distance. He can't make Montauk tonight. What he'll do is find a dry place, some potato shed or something, where he can stay until morning and then start out again.

He makes a left off Montauk Highway onto a road lined with potato fields. It looks familiar—somewhere near here his parents once rented a house. Through the rain he can barely see scattered sheds, barns, and farmhouses. Farther on, beyond a railroad bridge, there's one lone half-built house. The Moped sounds awful again, like a wet vacuum cleaner. He's got to get inside soon even if it's only for a while. This place should do it. The roof and walls are up. There's a No Tresspassing sign, but nobody will bother him in weather like this.

Rain is still falling. No door yet, so he drags the Moped across mud and shoves it through the doorway into the house. What's that sound? A sheet of plastic, covering a skylight, has come loose and is snapping in the wind like a sail or a flag. At his feet are wood shavings, lunch debris, and beer bottles. Dave takes off his backpack and drops it to the floor. Smells nice, like a combination of a camp cabin and a country bar. He unties his sleeping bag. He'll stay here all night.

During his first hour in the house the time doesn't drag too bad. Dave dries the Moped, fixes his things, takes off his wet clothes. Wandering around among the bare beams, he finds some beer in a bottle and drinks it. It's warm and rusty tasting, but it quenches his thirst. After he's dried off as well as he can, though, there isn't much to do except stand and watch the rain. It's practically dark. It's getting cold, too. He puts on his sweat shirt and roams from one part of the house to another, wondering what to do until it's time to go to sleep.

If it would only quit raining . . . if that damned flapping sound would stop . . . It's lousy, all of a sudden, being in this house. Dark and damp, reminds him of— No, he's *not* going to think of the accident now. Dave wanders into the bathroom and sits down on the edge of the tub. He can't help it—whenever he's alone, especially when it's rainy and dark . . . Jesus, what's that? He could swear it was Susan's voice.

You bought the car to impress me.

That wasn't the only reason!

You killed him—well, it amounts to that. . . .

I should have strapped him in with the belt!

You were watching me instead of the road.

I know it, I know it.

Just like that book we read in English—Tom and Daisy smashed people up. You expect to get off like they did?

"No, no, I don't. I'd do anything to make it right!"

Wait a second. Get control of yourself, man. He's talking out loud and nobody's here. Dave slides off the tub. He's left Belle Park and Susan. That's the point of coming here and starting a new life.

Shaking with cold now, all he wants is to be temporarily out of his misery. He gropes back to the spot where he left his sleeping bag. He crawls in. The house beams creak as he lies there unable to sleep. They won't let him alone—the people he's trying to lose. When he finally drops off, they come back in his dreams.

Susan smiles. "I like the way you drive." Jep appears like he always does, dead but not dead. Dave knows Jep shouldn't be there, but he doesn't want to scare him away, so he acts like it's natural that Jep has come back. Then, all too quickly, Jep's gone. "Come back," Dave calls, waking up in a sweat. What time is it? Four A.M. Oh, God, let morning come. He *can't take* dreams about Jep.

25

Dave rolls up his damp sleeping bag and starts tying it to the Moped. He looks outside, but he can't see much because of the fog. Two hours or more he must have lain here trying to fall back asleep. Hopeless. May as well get on with— Get on with what? On to Montauk. What for? Because he promised Jep he'd go there. But that was before the accident— Hey, no more *thinking* about that! What'll he do after Montauk? Worry about one thing at a time, jerk. Just get out of here now, if he can find his way through the fog.

Putting the backpack on his shoulders, he feels a V of pain. He wobbles as he drags the Moped out of the house. Man, he's weak. Can he do this? He hasn't eaten since noontime yesterday. The taste of stale beer is still in his mouth. He pees into the fog and then stands next to the Moped. The only sound he can hear is the coo of mourning doves. Get going. He straddles the bike. He can barely see where the road starts. Good bike, he tells it, flipping on its headlight. So weak he can barely see it. Good bike, find the road!

The bike finds it with some help from him. He keeps watching the line of gravel at the edge. After the railroad bridge, by the potato fields, he can hear sounds of tires from the highway ahead. Not much traffic this early, just the rattle and *whish* of trucks now and then. When he gets there, he stops and peers through the soupy, light-gray fog.

Everything's quiet. He crosses the highway and heads east. He can see just beneath him the white line at the edge of the road. The line in the middle—forget it. The only other thing visible is headlights coming toward him as cars round the bend. He rides on the shoulder to be on the safe side. Farther on the fog is patchy. He can detect buildings here and there—a motel, an antique shop. He should remember sometime to fill his tire with air. Now he steers back onto the hard surface just as a car silently passes him—near enough to let him feel a breeze as it goes. Close. He'll have to watch himself. Drivers can't see him. A thought idly pricks his brain. It'd be so easy to get hit. If he wanted to, that is. Hell, what's he thinking of? When he hears the next truck coming, he stays over on the right.

A cloud of fog lifts up ahead now, and Dave sees a service station. Air, he remembers. Better get some air here. Pulling off the road, he parks in front of the pumps. On the other side of the pumps he sees a gray van. The station is open—there's the attendant talking to some guy.

"Be right with you," he calls.

"I can do it myself," Dave says. "I just need some air."

"The hose is inside. Wait a second. I've got to bring it out."

Dave watches both men go into the station. He waits impatiently, jiggling. Finally he gets off the Moped and paces around the van. VERNON COOPER, CONSTRUCTION, REMODELING is painted on both sides of it. Dave remembers once dreaming of buying a van himself.

"Just a second," the attendant calls. "Sorry to keep you waiting!"

Dave paces around again. In one window of the van he sees a sign: HELPER WANTED and a number. Just then the attendant and the other guy come out of the garage.

The attendant, dragging a red hose, walks over to the Moped. "See you later, Vern," he says to the driver of the van. "Think it's going to clear up?"

"They say so, this afternoon." Vern looks at Dave. "Morning." He calls over to the attendant. "It *better* clear. The weather's put me behind. How's that bike on this road?" he asks.

"It's good," Dave says, nodding.

Vern shoves a shock of hair out of his eyes. "Well, I'd better be going. So long, Sal, I'll be seeing you."

Dave clears his throat. "That's you who wrote that ad—helper wanted?"

"Yeah," Vern says. "Why, you know somebody who might be interested?"

"I might be." Dave's pulse pounds.

"You're local?" Vern asks.

"Yeah." Dave watches the attendant fill his tire.

"Southampton?"

"Yes."

"What's your name?"

Dave hesitates. "Tobin. Paul Tobin."

"Don't think I know the name. What do your folks do?"

"They—aren't around. I'm on my own, actually."

"This wouldn't be permanent," Vern says quickly.

"That's okay," Dave says.

Vern waves at the van. "You see what I do. I'm remodeling a barn over in Bridgehampton right now, and I need a fellow to tear off an old roof. I might only need help for a week or two. You ever done anything like this?"

"I can do it," Dave says.

Vern looks at him appraisingly. "You'd be interested in working even today?"

"Yes."

"Well, I'm going there now. You can come with me if you want to, and I'll show you what's what. I usually get somebody I know, so I'd make this a trial. You could set your bike in the van here and drive over with me if you want to."

Dave can't believe the luck. "Okay," he says. "Thanks," he mumbles to the attendant. Meanwhile Vern opens the doors of the van, and Dave lifts the Moped in.

Squatting on the rooftop, Dave pulls up the hammer claw and frees a rotten shingle. He tosses it down below, where a pile is mounting up. Then he digs the claw in again, twists, and throws another one. Sweat drips from his forehead onto his bare chest. Laying the hammer down, he sticks his legs through the hole he's made and, hanging on to the main beam, lowers himself into the barn loft.

Dave glances at his watch. Eleven. Church bells are ringing—it's Sunday. He's been working almost four hours. The time has really flown. Looking out through the barn door, he can see Vernon carrying two-by-fours. Not a bad job, working outdoors like this, more or less on your own. Standing in the loft, he looks up at the roof, at all the shingles he still has to pull. There must be an easier way. Snooping around, he finds a crowbar and starts poking the shingles from underneath.

"Paul?"

It takes Dave a second to remember who he is. "Yeah?"

"What's going on?"

"I thought I'd try loosening the shingles from inside."

Vernon peers up from below. "You aren't hurting the beams, are you?"

"No. Wait, I'll show you." Dave gives the crowbar another upward swing.

"I'll be damned." Vernon smiles. "That could save us some time. What are you trying to do, hustle yourself out of a job?"

"No."

Vernon watches as Dave punches out a long row of shingles. "You got a good system there. Hold it, though, Paul. I could use some help moving lumber."

Dave joins Vernon outside.

"One, two, three," Vernon calls out, and together they lift the load. Near the house they put the lumber down. "Come here, Paul, I want to show you something." Vernon leads him through the back door into the house.

The kitchen has been gutted. Vernon points to two skylights. "Isn't this going to be something when it's finished?"

"Yeah, it's really nice."

Vernon runs his hand appreciatively over a smooth plank of wood. "The owner just said to me this morning he's got a friend wants some work done." He glances at Dave. "Maybe I'll be needing you longer. I see you're a worker, not one of these hand-me-something-for-nothing guys. From my end, it's going good so far. What do you think?"

"I agree," Dave says, following him out into the yard.

Vernon stands for a moment, examining the house. "Hey, I could use a cold drink—how about you?"

"Sure." For the first time Dave realizes he's still had nothing to eat.

Vernon takes a thermos out of the van and pours two cups of iced tea. Motioning Dave to join him, he sits on the grass. "How come you got all that gear with you?" he asks.

Dave glances at his backpack. "I camped out last night."

"Yeah?" Vernon's smile reveals big teeth. "Sounds pretty healthy to me. You don't have a car?"

"No."

"Well, maybe you're better off. You wouldn't believe the money I put into the van. You say you're on your own, Paul? Where do you live?"

Dave shifts. "I'm looking for a place—a room in a rooming house."

"You don't know anybody? No relatives?"

"No."

Vernon taps his fingers against the side of the cup. "I might know of a place. A neighbor of my sister's." Getting up, he puts the thermos and cups back in the van. "I'll find out tonight if that room's still for rent, Paul."

"Thanks," Dave says. "Guess I'll go back to work now."

"Just one thing first," Vernon says. "The deli will be crowded later on." He takes out his wallet. "How about going over there now and getting us a couple of sandwiches?"

Dave, taking the bill, tries to hide his eagerness.

"Ham and Swiss on rye for me, with mustard," Vernon says. "Get yourself something." He smiles. "I'm buying, so treat yourself good this time. You know which deli I mean—two blocks up on the left?"

"I'll find it," Dave lifts the Moped out of the van.

"Hey," Vernon calls. "Go ahead and take the van."

Dave looks at him.

"I mean it. You may as well get used to the feel of driving it. I'll be needing you to drive if you stay on with me."

Dave stands there stiffly, leaning on the Moped.

Vernon hands him the keys. "You never drove a van before?"

"No."

"But you've driven standard transmission?"

"Yeah—"

"There's nothing to it, then. I'll show you. Hop in." Vernon slides behind the wheel, and Dave slowly gets in beside him.

Vernon turns the key. "It might seem a little clumsy, but it's easy as one-two-three. Like this: reverse, low gear, middle, then high. Turn signals here, and over here is the horn." He honks.

Dave jumps.

"It's a loud son of a gun." Vernon smiles. "What do you think? Want to try it? Here, just take it down the driveway."

Vernon gets out and Dave climbs behind the wheel. *Do it,* he tells himself. He puts his foot on the clutch and his hand on the shift stick, but the second he takes the wheel, he realizes he can't.

"What's the problem?" Vernon asks.

"I'll ride the Moped, okay?"

"You know how to drive, don't you?" Vernon looks at him skeptically. "I'll be needing you to drive."

"Yes, I know how." Dave gets out of the van.

"And you have a license?"

"Yeah," Dave says, sitting on the Moped. "I'd just like to wait—until some other time."

"Well, you got to feel comfortable. Go on then," Vernon says. "Two blocks on the left. Ham and Swiss on rye."

"So long," Dave says distractedly. The Moped shimmies down the driveway. At the end of two blocks he passes the deli and keeps going. Vernon's right about feeling comfortable. Dave wishes he did, but he knows that he never will, behind the wheel of a car.

26

Bridgehampton is behind him. On the highway, going toward Montauk, Dave rides past fields and vegetable stands where people are buying corn. What if he can't find a job and keep it? What if he can't start over again? Don't think about it now. Get to Montauk, that's the main thing. At least he'll be away from *people* there. It's deserted where he's heading, at that certain great spot on the far side of the Point. Wavering slightly, he crosses the white line. Brakes screech and a car swerves.

"Jesus Christ!" the driver yells, slowing up and riding alongside him. "Watch where you're going!"

Dave tries to ignore him, an old guy.

"Those things ought to be banned! Where's you helmet? You're illegal!"

Dave stays on the shoulder until the guy moves on. Damn it, he's jumpy now. The old guy shook him up. Good, here's East Hampton. Not much farther to go. He can picture the spot at Montauk, at the bottom of a cliff. So private last year they could lie naked on the beach. Dave stops at a traffic light, feeling shaky as anything. He's hungry, that's it. If he's hungry, then *eat.* Fingering the bill Vernon gave him, he parks the bike in a bike rack and rushes into the first store he sees. "Ham and Swiss," he says.

The clerk gives him a look. "This is a hardware store."

Dave hurries out in embarrassment and goes directly back to the Moped. What's wrong with him—is he going nuts? Come on, keep on moving. For a minute he feels panicked. What's he doing here, anyway? He's keeping his promise. No, that's crazy. Crazy or not, he keeps going to the Point. Leaving town, he passes a sign that says CHI-NESE TAKE-OUT. Chinese food makes him think of Nan. He wonders if she's mad that he hung up on her. Where the dunes begin, out of Amagansett, he opens up the Moped and flies faster than he's flown since the beginning of the trip.

This is it then . . . almost there. Scrubby pines grow on both sides of the road. Now and then a car whizzes by. The lighthouse is up ahead. He passes the sign: *Montauk Point State Park,* and winds around toward the lighthouse. This is the crowded side of the place—tourists roaming all around, people with cameras heading down to the beach or over to the restaurant. The spot he's aiming for is nothing like this, here. He keeps riding on, around the end of the Point.

This is more like it. No buildings. Just miles of bushes, sloping down the hill. Somewhere around here is where they camped out the last time. He stops the Moped at the edge of the road and looks at the ocean. Man, the noise. And he forgot how *far down* it is. No way to find their old path from before. He'll have to push through the bushes all over again. And he'll have to leave the Moped hidden up here on top. He hates to leave it, but what can he do? He jams it into the bushes and, taking his sleeping bag, balances it on his backpack and starts going down.

Twigs snap under his feet and prickly branches scrape

his face. It's tougher than he figured—briars snag at his pack. Much harder than last year, when Jep went first and broke a trail for him. Damn it, little insects are flying up his nose. He goes on, though, protecting his head with his arms, as if he were scrimmaging against some dirty-playing team. Stomping the low bushes with his feet, he finally makes it to the bottom and comes out of the last tangle onto a strip of pebbly beach.

This is it. Maybe not the exact spot, but pretty close to it. Dave drops his gear and sits down on the sand. It's just as deserted as he remembered, completely hidden by underbrush. And just as wild as he remembered, the way the waves crash on those rocks. Gulls are crying and swooping. Dave sees what they're after—a pile of mussel shells glistens like coal on the beach. With each wave more black shells wash up and more gulls circle over. It's eerie in a way. No it isn't, it's nice.

It was nice last year, anyway. They brought a lot of stuff that time—six-packs and matches to build a fire on this narrow strip. Hell, nothing's the same this time. No food. No raunchy songs. No wild stories. Dave stands up suddenly. This time there's no Jep. What was the point of coming here? He must be trying to punish himself. Or maybe he's trying to bring back what was. He can't, Dave realizes, staring out past the waves at the place Jep insisted on swimming to show his fearlessness.

Dave stands for a moment mesmerized by the sound of the waves. Sweat drips off his forehead. May as well take a swim. He pulls off his sneakers and shirt and sticks one foot in the water. Colder than he expected. He goes in ankle deep. A wave booms farther out, spraying the rocks and his cutoffs. Water rises to his knees. Picking his way over shells, he can feel a place where the bottom drops off. Ducking, he submerges. At first the cold shocks him so bad he almost yells.

He swims a few strokes, his whole body tingling. Then he adjusts to the water and swims as hard as he can between two jagged rock pillars, but the waves beat him back. Regaining his footing, he stops to catch his breath. Hard to get beyond the waves. How did Jep do it? A huge one is building up now, a curved wall of water that could smash him like a shell if he landed on these rocks. He watches the wave crash. After that there's a lull. *Now.* He fills his lungs, and while the next wave is swelling, he dives under it. When he opens his eyes everything is dark green.

Surfacing quickly, he finds himself between the sets of waves. The outer set is arched and ready to spill. He dives again, but too fast, without enough of a breath, so that he comes up spitting water and gasping for air. Damn, he can't breathe! He inhales and coughs water up. But he made it, at least, beyond the second set of waves!

Over now, on his back. There—he floats with his back arched. The ocean swells beneath him, but gently, like he's on a raft. Filling his lungs again, he feels his legs rise until he lets out air and they sink. Too much muscle—he's not a floater. Not like Willo, for instance. Still, for the first time in a long time he almost feels calm here. With the swells lifting him slightly and water in his ears, weird sounds seem to be coming up from the ocean floor below. Hollow *pings,* like stones bumping—messages, maybe? What are they telling him? He lifts his head and looks around.

He sculls, facing shore. Jesus. He's pretty far out. He'd better swim back in quickly. He starts doing the crawl.

The first strokes get him nowhere. Kicking harder and pulling straight down with his arms, he goes at it again, but when he raises his head he feels like he's in the same place. Must be the wind or something, damn it. Now he thrashes like a caught fish. All that it gets him is his heart pounding fast.

And his chest feeling caved in. He stops swimming, treads water, and tries to catch his breath. Unless he's imagining it, the shore's getting farther away. What do you do? He tries to remember from lifesaving in junior high. Meanwhile the water's getting cold and he's worried about leg cramps. He floats on his back, hoping to save his breath, but it doesn't work out right, because water laps over his face and makes him sputter like mad. *What'll he do?* Straining his eyes, he can't even see his spot on the shore anymore. Even the rows of waves are getting pretty hard to see. The answer comes to him suddenly about what to do—nothing. He'll float and let what ever happens, happen, that's all.

He turns onto his back again and tries to be as calm as before. But he can't. Gulls are crying. He's crying, too. Not out loud, but inside. This isn't his fault. He never meant to, but now that it's this way, let it be. His life for Jep's. Evens things up, right? He always wondered what it would be like, how long it would take. Three minutes, he seems to remember, but that's after you go under. Will his whole life flash by him? Things are flashing by now. That's nothing new—since the accident he sees things. Relax, okay? Float. *It's out of his hands.*

Within a few minutes he can feel a swell rising that will wash over him completely if he stays in a float. *Let it,* he tells himself. *Give in to it, easy.* But as it comes, he lifts his head and treads water again. What's wrong with him, thinking of giving in? Stupid idiot, still trying to *prove* something? One mistake isn't enough? Quit trying to match Jepson—you did that before! The swell catches him anyway, so he swallows a mouthful of water. Spitting it out, he's determined to get back to shore.

Don't fight the pull. *Go* with it, on the diagonal. Who cares if he ends up far from where he left his gear? Heart pounding, he tries it. Maybe the wind's changed or something, because as long as he tacks in he's doing pretty good. Legs aching, though. Long way to go yet. What's coming toward him, a raft? No, a big blob of seaweed, this side of the waves. Huge swell underneath him now. Don't fight the undertow. Go with it, crosswise, no matter how long it takes. Do the sidestroke, less tiring. Foot cramping—watch it. He fills his lungs and kneads his arch until it starts to relax.

There, better. Seems like miles, but waves are finally coming up. He's not near where he started out. Watch those waves, tricky stuff. If he heads down the middle between those two big rocks over there, he ought to be able to ride the waves in and end up on the beach.

A swell raises him up suddenly. He's riding on the crest of a wave and spinning like a flywheel out of control. God, help! He churns downward, scalp scraping the bottom and then over and over in a wild somersault. No, please, don't let him taste it. Not so close to shore like this. His lungs fill with water as he's gasping for air. Chest feels caved in again. Head up, he coughs. The next wave whips him under, toward the rocks on the right.

Lost now. Where's Jepson? Dave gropes underwater. He's got to save him this time. This time he will. But another wave pulls Dave farther under and dashes him against a rock, so that, whimpering in pain, he can't see anything.

Floating. Facedown. Waves crashing around him. Jepson? I tried. Did all I could. Wanted to bring back both of us. Looks like I botched it. Jep, hey—forgive again?

Body weightless. Waves rippling over the backs of his legs now. Breeze on his shoulders. Cheek pressed in rough sand. Bed of nails? No, mussel shells, gouging his stomach. Don't move, or his head will split in two halves.

How long? No idea. Aching head slowly clearing . . . his face in the sand. Water laps his heels. Shadows long, like it's late. Rump cold, in wet cutoffs. He lifts his hand to his head and it comes away stained with red. He lies there on his stomach, trying to put it together. Tide must have gone out and left him on land. So *beat* . . . it's going to take all he's got to lift his head. Using every ounce of strength, he rolls over and sits up.

27

With his bare feet stinging, Dave climbs up the crude path through the bushes. Close to the top he crouches to rest. He shivers. Pretty cool now that the sun has gone down. His cutoffs are almost dry, but he doesn't have a shirt. Or sneakers. Or the rest of his stuff. Probably he should've gone looking for it, but he's worried about the Moped hidden up here. Plus spotting an actual path made his climb easier than going back from where he started from and using the trail. What'll he do if he can't find the Moped? What'll he do next even if he *can?*

Dave touches his forehead cautiously. The bleeding has stopped now. He must look like a wreck—he can feel a lump on his head. He still isn't sure how he made it in to shore. Maybe he's getting lucky. Standing on shaky legs, he keeps climbing up.

At the top he stands for a second trying to get his bearings. The sky has gone blue-gray with splashes of pink. The waves, with the tide out, seem like gentle little ripples. God, he's relieved to be standing here now. He's closer to the lighthouse than when he started swimming. That means the Moped is somewhere around the bend. He'd give anything to have his sneakers as he steps onto the road. But he'll have to wait until it's light in the morning to go down and look for them.

Meanwhile, he's not in such good shape—he's starving and his head aches. Maybe Vernon would take him back. Not that that's any help for tonight. He'll find the Moped and sleep out right there, where he hid it, and in the morning he'll climb down and pick up his stuff. Walking along the edge of the road, he tries to figure out how far the ocean carried him and where the Moped must be. Now that it's almost dark, it seems impossible that he'll be able to see it at all.

He walks for five minutes or so, checking the bushes. His feet are okay as long as he stays on the road. A couple of cars go by. In the beam of the headlights he can see how the road curves, and he has a strong hunch that he left the Moped near here. With the headlights gone he has to feel his way, which is painful to his hands and feet. Then, when the next car shines its lights, he almost yells out. There it is—the glint of the handlebars five feet away!

Grabbing the Moped, he tries to yank it out. He practically hugs it when it moves. It's on the road now, and he smiles at the familiar *putt-putt.* He'll take a little ride just to make sure it's okay and to see if somewhere he can find something to eat. At the park restaurant if it's still open. He feels in his pocket. The bill from Vernon is wet, but it's still there. While he's putting the bill back, a car pulls up behind him. At first he pays no attention, but then its lights start to flash. When he sees that it's a police car, he registers surprise, but instead of taking off, he watches the cop get out.

"Your license? May I see it?"

"I haven't got one," Dave tells him. "The Moped isn't mine." The cop is a young guy.

Now the cop moves in closer. "May I see your I.D.?"

Dave doesn't feel nervous. If anything, a kind of relief. "I don't have any on me. I lost my wallet last night."

"What's your name?" The cop studies the Moped and then looks at Dave.

"Dave Jacoby."

The cop nods. "Where do you live?"

"I'm from Belle Park. I've—been living in Belle Park."

"You always go around like you are now, half dressed?"

"No, my stuff is down there—on the beach."

"Sleeping on the beach isn't allowed here, you know." The cops looks at him hard. "What happened to your head?"

"I was swimming. I bumped it."

"How about if you come with me and we'll have it checked out."

"No, thanks," Dave says quickly. "It happened a couple of hours ago. If it was serious, I wouldn't be able to stand here and talk." The cop is staring him down.

"I'm going to have to take you in, sir," the cop says.

"Take me in?"

The cop nods. "There're a few things to clear up. First, they've got a wallet at the Southampton Police Department. If you can prove you are who you say you are, you can get your wallet back."

"Was it found at a Gulf station?"

"Could be," the cop says.

"Is the money still in it?"

"It should be worth your while coming in to find out. I'm from the East Hampton department, but I'll drive you over to Southampton. Let's leave the Moped here—I'll lock it up for you."

"I'd rather not leave it."

"It's not yours, you say?"

"No, but—"

The cop's eyes stay on his. "You'd like to see the owner gets it back?"

"Yeah." Dave looks at him. "Why, what do you mean?"

The cop pulls on his visor. "A couple of your friends are out here looking for you."

"Willoughby?"

"I think so. He's the one who owns the Moped?"

"Yeah. Where is he? How do you know—?"

"They were in touch with the Southampton Police Department yesterday. When they asked about a Jacoby, your wallet had just been turned in. Your friends were pretty worried about you—they still are."

The cop is giving him a look now, like he's expected to explain it all.

"They said you took off"—he waves his hand—"just like that. Do your parents know where you are?"

"They went away for a weekend. I left them a note."

"And you came out here—to camp?"

The cop is trying to be a nice guy. "Yeah," Dave says. "You've been *looking* for me?"

"Well, this is my area. I patrol here all the time. You happened to be the third person I've checked out. Your friends are in the park, by the way. I saw them about fifteen minutes ago."

"Here?"

"In the parking lot. It's about to close, but you might catch them. If we miss them, no problem—they said they were taking a room at the Sands Motel."

Dave pauses. "They? Who? Willoughby and who else?"

"I only talked to the big guy, but he said he was with

someone else. How about it—want to take a look for them?"

"Can I ride over to the parking lot?"

"As long as I follow you." The cop shines his flashlight on Dave's face again. "How'd you say you hurt your head?"

"Swimming. A wave knocked me down."

"It sure as hell did. Took your shirt right off, too, Okay, see you over in the lot. My name is Harkins."

"Thanks." Harkins put on his low beams and Dave rides in front of him between two shafts of light. Willo's here. How about that? Willo came all the way out here. Dave stops at the entrance to the parking lot, but he sees that it's closed.

Behind him, Harkins pops his head out of the window. "Looks like our timing is off. Your friend was driving a blue Chevy? That's the right guy, isn't it?" Harkins opens his door halfway so he can talk to him better. "Maybe you can catch up with him at the motel."

"Yeah."

"Go on—hit the highway. You shouldn't without a license, but I'll follow you over. Sands Motel, first one on the left." Harkins mumbles a few words into his car radio mike and then both of them take off toward the exit to the park.

Dave sticks close to the shoulder, the cop car behind him. He turns on the Moped's headlight. The wind off the ocean sends a shiver straight through him. Thank God he's here—what must that water be like now? Harkins gives oncoming cars a signal to turn their beams down, and at the first neon sign he overtakes Dave and pulls into the motel. Dave follows into the driveway and waits behind the police car.

Harkins leans out of his window as a man comes out of the motel office. "I'm looking for a Willoughby," Harkins says.

"Big guy?"

Harkins nods.

"Number twenty over there. I think they're in. Need any help?"

"No, no. It's nothing—routine. Don't disturb yourself." Harkins gets out of the car and the man goes back inside.

Dave wonders where Willo's Chevy is. He doesn't see it parked in front of the motel unit.

"Look." Harkins comes toward him. "Let's put it this way. I don't think it'll do anybody any good if I take you in tonight. How about this? Return the Moped to your friend, bunk in with him, clean yourself up, and stop by the station in the morning—Southampton, that is. If your friends identify you, you can probably claim your wallet." Harkins, shifting uncertainly, keeps looking at Dave. "You'll be okay once you're with them—your friends, I mean?"

"Yeah. Yeah, for sure."

"And your head is okay?"

"Yes."

"All right then. I'll wait in the car till they let you in. Any problem, call the department. I'm on till midnight. Tomorrow I'm in after four. I hope you'll be home by then." He pauses. "There's nothing going on here that I'm wrong to let go, is there?"

"No, it's okay. I'm okay." Dave offers his hand.

Harkins shakes it. "Good luck then. Go put a shirt on."

"Thanks again."

Harkins, nodding, slides behind the wheel and waits while Dave parks.

Dave walks up to number twenty. There's a light on in the unit, but where's Willo's Chevy? He must have left it in the back. Even though he's feeling good that Willo cared enough to come out here, Dave's shaking a little as he knocks on the door.

"Who's there?"

Dave steps back. The door opens a crack and he sees Nan's face. He can't help smiling at her expression. He's feeling pretty giddy anyway.

"Dave!" Nan's voice rises. "Where—? Oh, I'm so glad you're here!" She backs off to look at him. "How come—? Did Willo see you? He just went out. Oh, I'm so relieved—" She stops.

Dave comes a step closer and leans against her gently. "No, I didn't see him yet. Where did he go?"

"Out to get food."

"Food." He glances down at her. "I'm glad to see you, too. You have no idea how glad."

Nan looks up at him. "What happened?"

"It's a long story."

"No, I mean what happened to your head?"

"A rock got me." Dave touches the lump. "I went in the water near the Point this afternoon, and I almost— I had a close call."

She quickly meets his eyes. "It was an accident, you mean—?"

"An accident, yeah. Look, I'll try to tell you everything. Think we could sit down?"

Nan whirls around. "Sure, here, sit on one of the beds. Aren't you cold? Take my jacket." She plumps a pillow up. "It was Willo's idea to stay in a motel tonight. We got caught in the rain last night and our sleeping bags are soaked. We had just enough money—" She suddenly starts smiling. "I can't believe this. How did you find us? Did that policeman tell you where we were?"

"Yeah, Harkins picked me up at the park. Nice guy, a good guy." Dave sinks down on the bed. "How did you two get here?"

Nan pulls up a chair tentatively. "I hope—you aren't mad that I came—"

"No, no."

"Good." Nan hugs her knees. "The main thing, I was worried about *you,* but I was also worried that you'd be mad if we came looking for you out here. Willo's known you your whole life, but I'm—well, I thought you wouldn't want me to interfere."

"No, when I left I was annoyed. I still am at certain people, but not at you or Willo. I'm—I'm really glad you came. Willo went for food? Where did he go?"

"Close. He may have stopped at the police station one more time. We gave them a description of you. We thought—it doesn't matter now—let's just say . . . your wallet! Did you know your wallet was found?"

"Yeah."

"When we heard that, Willo took it as a good sign. It proved you were out here, but I was afraid," she says.

"I'm okay now, I really am." Dave waits until she looks up at him again. "When did you decide to come?"

Nan shifts in her chair. "When you didn't show up at football camp, Willo was positive something was wrong. He and the coach kept calling your house, and then Willo went home and saw the Moped was gone. He called me, and I told him what you had said about Montauk. We both had a feeling—"

"I didn't know I was coming here when I told you about Montauk."

"Well, we checked before we came. Willo called the police. I hope you don't mind that he did that, but just in case you were—you know, in trouble or something. Anyway, when he spoke to Southampton, they said your wallet had been turned in."

"So you came."

She nods. "Willo was glad to have company. We didn't tell anyone else except the coach." She pushes her hair back. "My father thinks I'm camping with a girl friend." She looks at him intently. "Are you sure you're all right?"

"Yes."

"Would you tell me if you weren't?"

"Yes, I would now."

She closes her eyes and then opens them again. "Swear?"

"I'll swear on a glass of water. Think you could bring me one?"

Nan keeps watching him as she gets up and goes to the bathroom sink. Then she brings him the glass and sits on the edge of the bed. "Here, don't move." She holds the glass to his lips. "Have you eaten?"

He shakes his head.

"Willo's buying food. It won't be long now."

Dave takes the glass in his hand. "I feel bad—" He breaks off. "Not that I came—I guess I had to do that. I had to get out of there for a while. But I feel bad that I messed up what you two were doing."

Nan looks in his eyes. "You left because of Susan."

Dave puts down the glass. "That and all this stuff on my mind that I couldn't tell anybody about. I tried to tell my parents . . . I almost told *you* the other day. *The accident was my fault.* I was arguing with Susan in the car just before it happened."

Nan puckers her mouth nervously. "You had been seeing her, right?"

"Yeah, sickening, isn't it?"

"But when we went to the concert, wasn't it over? You were disgusted with her that night."

"Yeah." Dave rocks forward. "I told her it was over. I would have explained everything to Jep the next day, but he got hung up at school. I had tried to tell him other times, but something always stopped me. Then Susan went ahead and told him herself." Dave lowers his head. "At first he wanted to fight me, but—" he sits up—"he *forgave* me, finally. That's how I took it anyway. I said, 'I'm sorry, man. *I'm sorry!*' And he said 'It's okay.' " Suddenly everything Dave has buried comes out in a shaking sob. Nan takes his hand, and he lets go of the tears that he's tried to hold back.

Nan squeezes his hand. "He cared more about you than he did about her."

"I guess so." Dave gets control of his voice. "Maybe he felt like I did—attracted but sick of her, both at the same time. Let me tell you the rest of it," he goes on, wiping his face with his hand. "I was arguing with Susan . . . Jep was zonked out." Dave can barely hear his own voice—it sounds like someone else's. "She was telling me to watch out, and that made me mad. If I'd listened to her, maybe . . ." Dave brushes his eyes with his hand. "I told her all she wanted was kicks, and that got *her* mad. She said Jep was more exciting than I am. I got annoyed. I don't remember much from then on. I may have speeded up. Or else I was looking at her in the mirror to see what she'd do next. I killed him." Dave pauses. "That's what she told me. Out of jealousy, she says. That part's a lie. I loved Jep. I'd have done anything for him. The worst part is, now there's nothing I can do to try to make it right."

"You'll just have to—"

"What, go on *living?*"

"Yes. Don't knock it."

"It could have been all over this afternoon," he says, slipping down.

"You didn't intend to—?"

"No, not actually, I started to swim out because I remembered Jep doing that when we were there the last time. See—still competing with him! I drifted farther than I expected and at some point it seemed easier just to keep going instead of coming back. It was just a flash—I didn't mean to. That's all my parents would have needed, right?"

"And your friends," Nan says quickly.

"Yeah." Dave nods. "You know what else has made all this so bad? Nobody blames me. Everybody excuses me, when I can't excuse myself. If they'd sent me to *jail* it would have been easier."

"But since they didn't," Nan says, "you've been jailing yourself."

"Yeah, I guess so." Dave sighs. "How long will it go on? For the rest of my life?"

"I hope not," Nan says.

"*Time,* I know." Dave falls back. "God, make this year go fast. No, I take that back." He exhales. "It goes quick enough."

Nan puts her head down until it touches his chest.

"Have you thought about how crazy it is that *you* were the one it happened to, when Jep was so famous for drinking and showing off?"

"Yeah." Dave's voice is hoarse. "I guess there isn't always logic. One slip is all it takes. It's going to kill me to drive again. Like it kills me every time I hear the word *kill*. I'll have to drive, I guess, sometime. And face Susan again."

"School's day after tomorrow." Nan raises her head.

Dave looks at her. "Have you made your decision yet?"

"About Gloria? I think so."

"Maybe we should both leave Belle Park and start from scratch out here," Dave says.

Nan smiles. "Don't say that. I might take you up on it."

"That'd be okay." He takes her hands now. "What did you decide?"

"I'm telling my father it's okay for Gloria to move in. One more year is all I'll be there, but their life will go on. She's not a witch or anything. Don't you think it's the right choice?"

Dave nods. "Come to think of it, I wish she were here now—with an order of ribs and rice, lemon chicken, what else?"

"A shirt with a label. What happened to your shirt?"

"It's with the rest of my stuff on the beach near the Point."

"Don't you want it?"

"To tell you the truth, I'd just as soon leave it there. Nan?"

"Yes?"

"Think I should tell anybody else about all this?"

"About feeling it was your fault?"

"Yes."

"Your parents? From everything you've said, it seems like they really want to help. You wanted to tell them before. Why not tell them now?"

"And then tell the cops?"

"See what your parents say."

"I can't wait." He sits up impatiently. "I want to get home before they do on Tuesday, to take back this note I wrote. Is that Willo?" he asks, looking out the window at the sound of a car.

Nan nods.

Dave leans forward until their foreheads meet. "Thanks for coming to look for me. I'm going to get through this year somehow. You'll be around, won't you? You won't go back to California?"

"No."

They get up from the bed.

"Nan!" Willo's voice carries. "He's here, isn't he? I see the Moped!"

Nan opens the door.

Willo, rushing in, drops a pizza carton on the floor. "Jacoby!" Willo comes at him with his arms outstretched. He stops. "Man, what *happened?* Who beat you up?"

Dave slaps Willo's palm and then squeezes his hand hard. "The main thing is I'm here and I'm still in one piece. Thanks for doing all you did—missing camp and everything. It's really good seeing you."

Willo grins. "Hell, that's more words than I've heard you say in weeks. Are you sure— I *knew* we'd find you— Are you *sure* you're okay? I'm calling the coach. You look like you've been through ten weeks of football camp. Where've you been? I missed the whole story, right?"

Dave nods. "I'll tell it over again for a piece of that pie."

"The man's hungry!" Willo swoops down and opens the carton.

Dave feels dizzy as the aroma of pizza fills the room. He takes the first piece with shaking hands. "Thanks. What do you want to know?"

"I'll give you a break." Willo hands him another piece. "Eat first and talk later. Okay, Nan, here." He gives her a slice of pizza. "You can talk while I'm driving, Jacoby."

Both of them look at him.

Willo takes a big bite. "I'm for going home as soon as we eat."

"Fine with me," Nan says.

Dave eats the pizza ravenously. "Whatever you two want to do is okay with me. What about my wallet? I have to stop in Southampton."

Willo gives him the next slice. "No problem. Or with the Moped—it'll fit in the trunk. I can go to camp tomorrow if we get back tonight."

"So will I," Dave says.

"Are you kidding? Not with that beat-up head. Jeez, I forgot the sodas—here. Lucky I got an extra." Willo, pulling tabs, hands one to each of them and lifts his to his lips. "Here's to—whatever."

The hissing sound reminds Dave of afternoons at Jepson's. No amount of time is going to wipe out the pain. "Here's to you two." He clears his throat. "Thanks for coming to get me. I've got an awful lot to deal with yet, but I feel better that you came." His hand wobbling, he raises the soda can. "Here's to friends and to me finding a way to do something good now to balance the bad. I think I can do it. Damn it, I will."

This book may be kept

FOURTEEN DAYS

A fine will be charged for each day the book is kept overtime.

MAR 17			
SEP 21			
EP 20			
GAYLORD 142			PRINTED IN U.S.A.